Praise for Michael Frost Beckner
&
SPY GAME

"Pass the popcorn!"
—*Amazon Editors' Pick*, Vanessa Cronin, Sr. Editor

"Brilliantly executed...First-class spy novels with a smart, gritty atmosphere."
—Charles Cumming, *New York Times & Sunday Times Best-selling Author of KENNEDY 35 and BOX 88*

"A thinking man's thriller... A real adrenaline blast... I loved it!"
—Robert Redford

"There's nobody quite like Beckner. Cerebral and unvarnished...with dialogue so sharp it's like dancing on hot coals. You'll swallow this book whole."
—I.S. Berry, *Edgar winning Author of THE PEACOCK AND THE SPARROW, A New Yorker & NPR Best Book of the Year*

"Michael Frost Beckner serves up a judicious blend of showy action, political intrigue, ticking-clock suspense, and CIA one-upmanship for mainstream entertainment."
—*Variety*

"There is nothing like *The Aiken Trilogy*... Laced with absurdity & stylistically daring ... Beckner [is] a razzle-dazzle showman at the top of the thriller heap."
—Editor's Pick, *Publishers Weekly*

"Beckner is one of the most unabashedly duplicitous writers I've ever encountered ... Brilliant work."
—Stephen England, *Best-selling Author of the SHADOW WARRIOR Series*

"Michael Frost Beckner is the rarest of spy novelists, a beautiful and compelling writer who also has a mastery of tradecraft and a deep understanding of how espionage really works."
—Joe Weisberg, *former CIA Officer and EMMY Award-winning creator of The Americans*

ALSO BY MICHAEL FROST BECKNER

HITLER'S LOKI
Berlin Mesa

SPY GAME
The Aiken Trilogy
Muir's Gambit
Bishop's Endgame
Aiken in Check

KALEIDOSCOPE:
A SPY GAME SERIAL
4th of July
Birthday
Halloween

A NATION DIVIDED
Volume I: Episodes 101-104
Volume II: Episodes 105-108
Volume III: Episodes 109-112

Kaleidoscope

A Spy Game Serial
Part 3:

Halloween

Michael Frost Beckner

MONTROSE STATION PRESS

Las Vegas
2024

Copyright © 2024 by Michael Frost Beckner

All rights reserved.

Published in the United States Montrose Station Press LLC

LIBRARY OF CONGRESS CONTROL NUMBER: 2024917067

ISBN 9798990351752 (paperback)
ISBN 9798990351745 (ebook)

'Paul Revere's Ride' by Henry Wadsworth Longfellow, 1864, in the Public Domain

Printed in the United States of America

Jacket Design & Illustrations by Andrew Frost Beckner

FIRST EDITION 2024

For John, my brother

KALEIDOSCOPE:

HALLOWEEN

"An ordinary fellow, who did not spend half his life torturing himself by trying to discover what was right so as to conquer his inclination towards what was wrong, might have cut the knot which brought their ruin."

—T. H. White, *The Once and Future King*

Prologue

Dìng dīng jīngshén.

A disposition.

An ethos.

The indomitable will of the worker to toil zealously, beyond the best efforts of their task. Toil until they embrace their work like the hammer embraces the nail.

钉钉精神

More than Party slogan, to Cheng Li-Qiang—the *zhèngwěi*, political ideology liaison attached to Shanghai Oceana Engineering Corporation (SOEC), a privately owned Chinese heavy construction and infrastructure firm—*dìng dīng jīngshén* was an absolute of his identity. It was bloodstream. It was sacred.

Dìng dīng jīngshén: The Spirit of Driving Nails. The anvil song that composed each beat of Cheng Li-Qiang's heart. It was China.

In December, and without fanfare, Cheng and a handful of SOEC engineers with a modest construction crew arrived at Woody Island—an inconsequential strip of reef and shoal in the Paracel archipelago in the South China Sea.

SINCE THE SECOND WORLD WAR, every nation bordering the South China Sea had jostled with every one of their maritime neighbors to lay claim to Woody Island, that sand-scruffy little patch of sea rock, but none of them wanted to put any committed effort into establishing true sovereignty. They tried to outdo each other with strongly worded proclamations. Taiwan drafted theirs. Indonesia wrote a good one. South Vietnam. North Vietnam next (and generously, as they proclaimed Woody Island for their allies, the Chinese). After the Vietnam War a unified Socialist Republic of Vietnam tore up their previous two and occupied the place.

This annoyed the People's Republic of China, who took a day out of 1974 to slaughter the ninety-four Vietnamese soldiers encamped on the island, followed by the drafting of the fanciest "From this day forward..." proclamation of them all. Woody Island, and all the sand spits of jaggedy teeth in the Paracel island-chain smile, would smile only for the PRC. The rest of you, think not? Try to knock out a tooth.

Technically, no one recognized China's claim. Like Vietnam, China never established permanent year-round habitancy. Whole thing was a big "who cares?" for the next thirty-nine years.

Woody Island, quietly baked in the tropical sun.

A single Five-star Red Flag on an unimpressive pole snapped in the sea wind next to a cluster of small administration buildings the Chinese never upgraded from earlier French Indochina occupation. Seagulls saluted the flag more than any human ever did and for four decades the tides rolled, and the fish grew fat. Woody Island became an itinerant home for Chinese fishermen; for meteorologists and oceanographic researchers; light-duty contract work for air and marine traffic controllers who came and went on lazy rotations.

But now it's 2011—December, so almost 2012—and Cheng and SOEC arrive. It's a little weird. On one hand, the dominant world superpower, the United States of America, has encouraged (to the point of economic coddling) China to walk out some private industry footprints worldwide. Gonna capitalism them out of communism. Watch and see. But this? Here? Aw, well, what's one little "his man Friday," Robinson Crusoe footprint on a remote fisherman's beach? Give 'em a Tiki bar. Hadn't the international community, including China's whiney neighbors, been raising their voices and pointing at all those proclamations and international obligations written in ink that clearly stated recognition of sovereignty only exists once a permanent population is in place? Turns out, China was fulfilling the obligation none of the others had been willing to do and writing it in red ink.

When the SOEC civilian crews launched construction, the international community was wary, but hard-pressed to find fault.

A movie theater.

A shopping center.

An apartment complex.

Oh, and off to the side—hardly relevant—a teeny-tiny cluster of new administration buildings. An afterthought. Like, "Come on, really?"

The tide rolled. The fish grew fat.

Bolstering this look-the-other-way attitude, for the past three years, US Armed Forces and their intelligence brethren who monitored these things found less to monitor as military traffic between the mainland and Woody had decreased to its lowest level since 1999.

SOEC completed the shopping center and movie theater in March. They shipped the film *Flying Swords of the Dragon Gate* from the mainland. Screened it in celebration.

The mockery of the sailors on the *USS Ronald Reagan*, fifteen nautical miles off the island's coast, made clear their condescension for the Chinese movie premiere (a year-old chop-socky everyone had already seen) when they screened *The Avengers* a month *before* its release. Inside a hangar bay with twice the seating. With thirty F/A-18 Hornets lined behind them. Not to mention the twenty fighters on the flight deck above and ever-ready to go. So, *woot-woot* Woody Island.

Sansha (meaning, "Three Sands"—how quaint) would be the People's Republic of China's smallest city; its least populated prefecture. The West, along with their East Asian allies, took this unaggressive, all mouth no swallow move by China as encouragement that the ever-expanding, ensnaring loops of their hegemonic dragon coils had reached the limit of outward expansion.

Then someone who wasn't an idiot did some math.

Sansha City—on its one eighth of a square mile coral reef and sandy shoal—controlled over 800,000 square miles of maritime territory.

That's called an F-ing big deal.

On April 08, 2012, three hundred seventy-five miles away—that point in a magic show where the magician extends his arm and jazz hands his fingers wide and empty-palmed as far away from his other hand as possible—a Philippine Navy BN-2 Islander maritime surveillance plane identified eight Chinese commercial fishing boats at anchor off the Philippine-claimed Scarborough Shoal.

♔ ♔ ♔

CHENG HAD A BIT OF A SECRET. He wasn't *really* a political official keeping government tabs on a private industry endeavor. Cheng Li-Qiang was undercover for the Military Intelligence Bureau. He silently, and, trying his best, humbly, held the rank of Captain of the People's Liberation Army (Navy). But that day, upon receiving radio intercepts that the Philippine Navy dispatched patrol ship BRP *Gregorio del Pilar* posthaste to investigate Scarborough Shoal, Cheng gave in to a rush of pride unlike any he ever experienced. How his cheeks, his ears, burned; how his broad smile, inflamed with rays of personal pride, beamed...at all the men around him.

Appalled, ashamed. Humiliated. He abruptly exited the comms/code room inside the new administration center. Retreated to quarters. Fasted to cleanse himself of egotism. Of the bitter folly of self-aggrandizement.

He read from Mao.

Read the speeches of Xi Jinping, First Secretary of the Chinese Communist Party and Vice President of China—the moving force behind the Cabbage Strategy to which Xi had assigned Cheng responsibility for planning/implementation of this, its South China Sea opening ploy.

Three days later, Cheng emerged. Pride obliterated. Humility refreshed. Kept himself nominally abreast of developments at Scarborough but, having war-gamed every step with his staff—he credited them equally in the operation's design, ask anyone—already knew the chain of events that now would follow.

The Filipinos boarded the Chinese fishing boats. Attempted arrest of the Chinese fishermen.

Three Chinese Navy reconnaissance vessels blockaded the *Gregorio del Pilar*.

The Filipino boarding parties captured. Returned to their beleaguered ship.

The Philippine nation escalated; sent a destroyer.

And while Cheng, refreshed and ego-cleansed, would never claim credit for the second phase (his own singular idea), a cyber war erupted between the two powers. Public websites of both nations were defaced. Chinese and Filipino newspapers crashed. University electronic infrastructures in Beijing and Manila, tit-for-tat, infected the other with viruses; schools shut their doors.

Students flooded streets.

In China, the Shenjiamen Fishing Port navigational systems flatlined. A power grid collapse in Batangas City, Philippines, shut down the International Port.

Demonstrations flashed into riots.

Spread like wildfire from Hong Kong to Quezon City and all of it, on both sides: instigated by a single team of hackers in the service of the Chinese Ministry of State Security. (All Cheng, but he never bragged about it.)

Aggressor and victim muddled. Anyone who involved themselves—and, thanks to the Chinese Ministry of State Security, all the Southeast Asia nations did—hit each other with fishing bans. Embargos. Economic sanctions stretching from Beijing to Ho Chi Minh City, from Brunei to as far away as Florida in the United States where communist Cuban infiltrators, dutiful to Beijing, forced American commercial fishing strikes.

Captain Cheng Li-Qaing had risen from the lowest ranks of the *lau baixing*, the common people, by sheer determination. Academic brilliance. Physical excellence. Faithful discipline to the Communist Party ideology. A flawless subjugation of his ego. He tuned his heart to the spirit of *dìng dīng jīngshén*.

Under the cover of the Huangyan Dao Incident (as the Scarborough standoff became known), at Woody Island, Cheng took command over the SOEC project.

A series of rapid feats of engineering: the extension of the 1,200-foot runway by 3,000 feet to accommodate long-range heavy bombers; the clandestine deep-water dredging of the harbor to accommodate 5,000-ton warships; construction of a permanent military compound; the erection of barracks capable of housing a fully equipped force of 1,000 combat ready soldiers and sailors. Thirty-six years of age, Cheng Li-Qiang was an F-ing nail gun firing on automatic.

♔ ♔ ♔

ONE ACHIEVES THE BEST EFFORTS of *dìng dīng jīngshén* by the setting an example for the workers. Workers with an exemplar drive their nails more swiftly. More efficient-ly. Observable vigor and with joy. To set examples, a leader must make examples. By mid-August and halfway through the military construction, workers' passions for "hammering" seemed to Cheng to have dwindled.

Cheng Li-Qiang set four examples: a SOEC execu-tive vice president—to exemplify the sense of belong-ing one derives from sustained loyalty; a commander of Navy engineers—to illustrate the serenity/well-being derived from project security; one SOEC project man-ager to promote increased productivity, and another, well-liked, a funny-guy—sang Britney Spears when he got loaded—because Britney Spears is uncivilized. Tox-ic to Chinese character. All of them rousted at night. Taken at gunpoint under Cheng's bright-boy eyes, never to be seen again. *After* being seen tossed into the sea from an SOEC helicopter.

All projects were completed four weeks early, with surreptitious celerity. Now September, Cheng relayed to the mainland: "The People's Republic of China may set up local military command organs in Sansha City in full compliance with and according to relevant international regulations."

AT THE DINNER commemorating the transfer of mili-tary command from Captain Cheng Li-Qaing to Senior Colonel Cai Xihong, where Senior Colonel Liao Chaoyi was named Political Commissar, Cheng received an ur-gent summons the moment before he was to be recognized for his service; he bowed his way from the banquet hall. No one dared watch him leave.

A contingent of armed military police awaited. Escorted Cheng to the Senior Colonel's aircraft. His heart hammered. He clenched his jaw. What transgression could he have possibly made? The muscles bunched almost as large as the bold cheekbones that dominated his features, hard plateaus to set his eyes, dark as volcanic cinder, alert and calculating.

"Sit, Captain."

A white leather chair. Empty. Took it. Faced across a high-gloss black, carved table, a matched chair where his supreme commander studied him with a narrow, unfeeling smile.

"I am not here to congratulate you, Captain." He lifted his hand, revealing a scrap of paper. Three characters written upon it.

万花筒

"When we use a hammer to drive in a nail, a single knock is often not enough; we must keep knocking until it is well in place. Then we can proceed to knock the next one and continue driving in nails till the job is completely done. If we knock here and there without focusing on the nail, we may end up squandering our efforts altogether."

"I have made every effort to embody this."

"Truly." The supreme commander tapped the writing with his well-manicured index finger. Thin eyes bore into Cheng. He nodded at the paper.

万花筒 "Kaleidoscope," Cheng read out loud.

"A special project that is knocking here and there. A strong, steady hand is required on the hammer. To assume control. To set the proper example."

"I am yours to command."

"Then understand. It is the turn of the globe I am commanding you to."

Summer

1.

A SUMMER OF SIGNS and portents. Four hundred dead tobacco doves appear one June morning on the west thirty acres of yellow Orinoco. Blood rains from the sky on the seventeenth of July. August second, the devil appears inside a split log when slaves chopping wood see his grinning face in the matching sides. That night, eight haystacks combust in three neighboring parishes. On the roofs of the tobacco sheds, lanky, white-faced barn owls appear at midday the whole of an August week. They strut. Shriek. Would rather die than be chased by boys hurling rocks. And if August has been hot—and everyone agrees it is the hottest August in memory—overnight, on September the eighteenth, the temperature plummets.

From the manor house to the negro cabins, it is as if the broiled, sweat-bitter air of summer's expiration is all at once last-gasped through the chimney tops. With a horrid moan, an arctic beast insufflates its frigid breath into every space a creature lives. Explosion and crash. A thundersnow descends.

It will last for three days and become known in Maryland history as "The Autumn Witch of 1704." But the event most remembered by those who lived it—that strange and diabolic summer at Foxtail Farm—is Black Tom Brawny's wild escape from Claypoole Plantation.

With Black Tom Brawny's bloody scalp in fur-mitted fist, the legend of Turkey John Swann is born in horror.

♛ ♛ ♛

INSIDE HIS OFFICE on the ground floor of the North Vista Outhouse, Sylvanus Kingston does not rise from behind his desk as the buckskinned, pelt-bundled Piscataway Indian answers his boss' summons. In knee-length, sealskin moccasins, Turkey John Swann trudges to the fireplace.

Turkey John Swann lives with his Christian wife and three half-breed daughters in apartments above the Foxtail Farm wharf house. A former red-skinned slave himself, now manager of the Silas Kingston Sr.'s estate, he hires out across the colony as a tracker of runaway slaves. He stands in front of the raging fire, cooking himself on the double spit of his legs.

Silvanus Kingston waits while Turkey John heats his front, turns, and scorches the wet leather across his back to steaming. Then, the first Silas Kingston speaks.

"How high now?"

"Thirty-two inches in the fields."

"Will I lose it all?"

"A day more of this—a'least. More'n likely two." *Weighs his thoughts. "T'were a mean summer, boss, but more'n half the leaf is already in. Won't be hurt none in the drying sheds. The flues. Lest a roof crushes under*

the weight of the snow. What's left to harvest—?" Hard focus. "God's will."

"It shouldn't be snowing."

"It should if it is."

"You mustn't do this. He's not my property. I'm sure he's frozen dead of exposure. Reclaim him after the melt. A third of the reward, Mr. Claypoole would still pay."

"He's strong." Iroquois spike tomahawk on hip. "Brain-broke but smart." Coiled whip across his breast. "He's alive. He's running." No pistols. Snowshoes across his back. "I need this'n, boss."

"You mean to take him alive?"

"If'n Claypoole wants him an example."

"There won't be a trail."

"There is always a trail."

"It's foolhardy. I could order you not to."

"Don't."

"I can't afford to lose you."

"You won't. Do I have your permission?"

"Can I not persuade you to wait?"

"The infant child will not wait."

"If it isn't dead already. There is no woman who will take it. Foolhardy, this." He lets his words hang in the warm breath of the room.

"Silas. I want it."

Silvanus Kingston notices the exposed skin on Turkey John's face is thick with pig tallow. It glistens yellow in the firelight and matches the color of his tobacco-stained teeth. He appears the monster Christian folk already believe him to be. Silas nods consent.

Turkey John rotates again to absorb more of the fire's exhalation.

Silvanus Kingston looks out the window. Snow hurls, emptying in milk buckets from every direction. "Turkey John?"

The scalphunter grunts.

Silvanus doesn't turn. "What does it mean when the snow comes with thunder? I've never experienced this before." He shakes his head, mystified. "In summer, no less."

When the man doesn't answer, Silvanus turns around, but Turkey John Swann is gone.

♔♔♔

NO PATH. NO TRACKS. No vision beyond the tomahawk in the hand in front of his face. No geography: three feet of snow gives equality to the landscape. Against trees and boulders, drifts pile to heights of five, six feet. This matters not to Turkey John Swann. For three hundred years before the white man arrived, Turkey John's people lived, hunted, traded in this forest. The flats through the table rock—away from the hidden, secret hollows, the labyrinthine marshes—are the most strenuous path from Claypoole's farm and the most exposed, but the flats are fastest to make distance. Maximum distance is Black Tom Brawny's objective. Turkey John Swann mushes doggedly through the snow.

After three hours, he finds a trail of snow-fall-smoothed dips. Vanishing footprints. He increases his pace, moving faster than the snow can fill them. Within an hour, the staggered prints reveal crisp defini-tion along their edges. Thirty minutes later, the runaway slave's tracks are corn starch crumbling fresh. Ten minutes more, the Piscataway brave stands over his quarry.

"Reapoke," Devil, Turkey John mutters in his native language at the sight of the freezing West African.

Broad gunnysack covered back against a granite wall. Given up. Babble through teeth-chatter. Crazed and baleful eyes tilt upward. "Don't let 'em hang me."

"They aren't going to hang you."

Those eyes— Hope?

"I am. On your feet."

"Don't. I could'un face no one. Kill me now. Right here."

"Die the beast you've become? No. What you've done, you've done as a man. You will die and face men and your maker as that man."

Black Tom Brawny explodes in shakes and tears and wails. "I'm sorry! I'm sorry! Devil take me, I'm sorry!"

"I'm not. I'll take pleasure in cutting your scalp."

Turkey John hauls him to his feet.

Returns him to his master.

Claypoole: "Hang him."

Turkey John Swann scalps Black Tom Brawny as his rope strangles the man to death, swinging, head pouring thick red blood. Sky pouring thick snow, white.

♛♛♛♛♛

THE ISSUE OF REWARD. Claypoole confused. Bottom of the plantation house, snow-piled steps. "Thing's in the cabin. It is dead. What you've done's worth more than trash. Take the money you've earned."

"Dead or alive, the birth is what I claim."

"I'm not sure how I feel about this. Silvanus?" Claypoole's eyes appeal to his neighbor standing beneath the portico, receiving the heat rolling through the open front door.

Turkey John: "I don't want your money, Claypoole. I've earned my reward."

"Silvanus? You are my witness to this."

A distracted, "Yes?" And, noticing— "It's finally stopped. The snow."

Claypoole: "The baby is dead."

"If it is what Turkey John wants, I suggest you accede to his wishes."

Claypoole drinks from a brandy flask. Stares at the tomahawk. The scalp. Fresh and wet-red, tied to the Indian's belt.

"Go on, now. Take it. Our business is complete."

♛♛♛

SNOW BLOWS AROUND HIS BACK. Over seal-furred shoulders. Turkey John Swann shoves through the plank door. Enough blood that its cold iron smell fills the air after it has frozen. Frozen before it could seep into the dirt floor. Frozen on the frozen hide window cover. Frozen, glistening upon wall logs and clay chinking. Blood sparkles in icy crystals along the scythe blade tossed upon the empty pallet bed.

The slave woman of Black Tom Brawny waits where he abandoned her before he fled. Waits without patience. Waits without urgency. Known as Patty. Known for a sunny disposition. Known for a soaring laugh. Unknown, un-met in life by Turkey John, she waits in pieces of frozen human meat, human bone and her guts flung around the single room.

Turkey John locates her severed head in a corner. Patty's eyes are open but lost of the terror her last minutes in this world held. Stare without seeing her newborn daughter. Tucked inside a washtub right in front of her frozen eyes.

Turkey John Swann recognizes—as Black Tom Brawny did before he ran—the true father of the child by its pale skin, the pale-gray clay pools of the infant's unblinking, half-open eyes.

True to Silvanus Kingston's words, no one claimed the newborn child. But someone has cared for it. Some kind, but frightened soul cleaned the baby. Swaddled the baby. Packed the washtub with fire-heated bricks still warm to the touch, to keep this baby alive.

She breathes. She smacks her lips.

"Kuwumáras, nunutánuhs." I love you, my daughter.

She returns home with Turkey John Swann.

Reared by him and Pru, his white Christian wife, as their fourth daughter, she grows precious. She grows lovely of spirit and of sight to all who know her. Know her sunny disposition. Hear her heart-blooming laugh, her love for the world and for all family, friends, neighbors and strangers. Equal and alike. While throughout her life she is called "The Gift of the Devil's Summer," she is named Nika by her adopted heathen father—short for Nikamon—*which in the Algonquin language of the Piscataway People means both song and melody.*

2.

S UMMER SMOLDERED FOR THE Kingstons. A fire, intense, that never leaped to flame. As July baked to its end, the hole in Lynn's throat shrunk. Its oval edges, fat and fuchsia, moist and weeping, eyelids over an empty socket.

Sometimes at night, as the struggle of the day, the purgatory of her new assignment—her new Division transfer on a "medical/limited duties" Human Resources ticket—abandons Lynn to darkness, the darkness where she relives the Dulles Airport scissors that almost killed her; the darkness of her first direct contact with Kaleidoscope; and Lynn wraps herself in loneliness and self-recrimination.

In true Kingston form, Lynn—eyes shut, mouth shut, throat shut by her thumb—holds her breath and suspends/neutralizes her mind. A true Kingston, she forfends psychological/spiritual introspection and runs out of air on the litany of names of those she's failed:

Michael, Hal, Gary...

Her brain freeze-frames each face.

Father Cevik.

Helene Favre. Whoever she was.

Leigh. Russell Aiken. Doris.

Herself.

(The summer child she once was; the woman of eternal spring she had hoped to become, but failed.)

Lynn gasps awake. Lies discontented. Disconnected. Breathes and counts to the sound of each breath.

How odd. How dead to listen to my breathing from below my head. As if it isn't me.

The days burn. Nights boil.

And how, toward the end of her physical healing, the P/M valve removed, but before full decannulation, the hole whistles.

Phffssee-ffsss, phffssee-ffsss. Faintly horrific.

Reminds Lynn of her lips—when air once passed between them—youthful, berry-bright. None of the pinch of adult dissatisfaction; a puckered blow across the rim of a bottle of clambake beer. *Hwoo-Hwoooo.*

Chipped-polish, teenage toes curled in sand and seashell muck.

Phffssee-ffsss, phffssee-ffsss. Her throat-hole mimics the fluted moan of wind across the Foxtail Farm chimney top.

How much of the simple beauty of life we associate with breath? The first ticklish puff onto your newborn daughter's nose. The birthday candles you blow together with that daughter-now-niece, smoke curled, wisping away above pink icing on Leigh's first cake. Before Gwen's *"Let's better not do this next year. Don't we think?"*

The breath you catch after some man/*that* man kisses you and makes you breathless; the pairing breath you shared. Bodies pressed. Legs entwined in bed. Even if the only time it counted was once and now your breath is paired forever in a child you've by word and signature promised never to tell.

Phffssee-ffsss, phffssee-ffsss. Phffsseee...

Where is the breath that bursts from the center of your face those countless times you laughed, you cried, you gasped and sighed and felt the universe enter and leave you, sunny-warm-hopeful? Your living, breathing head where life once attached, three-in-one, mind, and body to the soul.

What soul?

Lynn's breathing, this sweltering summer, most resembled the breath of Foxtail Farm. The chimneys, as the seasons changed, and the *whoosh* of backdraft as her mother immolated and apotheosized. Not to the status of godliness, but to the strange and fallen angel she might have always been.

And then it would be daylight. Lynn would listen to the snake-hiss of her throat. *Phffssee-ffsss, phffssee-ffsss.*

August seared.

The dark cavity at wound's center contracted. The interior tissue fused, bubblegum pink and tacky. The outer flesh puckered. Closed over the hole like a sea anemone closes into itself. All that remains: a weal at the center of her jugular notch. Rose petal pink. The once-size of her baby's nose. Hard to notice. Unless—like Melody's twins—you stared. Hard to believe it had ever been and had ever separated her from the place of vision, sound, smell, taste, and thought, where "living," resides as experience.

Back at work in her white psych ward-like office, Lynn added the scarlet piece of beach glass, Paige had given her, to the vase on the corner of her desk. She waited to be moved to the Foreign Resources section of the National Resources Division. Waited her way through August.

On paper, I outrank my new division manager. Bitch fears me.

Waited into a September parched bone-dry as the summer humidity, awful and familiar, left the air, swallowed in a convulsion of summer's ashes burning out.

Gary Gravin rarely spoke to Lynn. Except to encourage patience and healing, and always *"Feel free to make it an early day."* But Lynn found her way—welcomed though uninvited—into the NR/Foreign Resources staff briefings inside the New Headquarters Building. She walked out (not to anyone's pleasure, but in her right) with potential foreign target dossiers, her new division manager's voice trailing, guarded and dissuading— "None of them are going anywhere, Kingston. Feel free to take your time. By fall we'll find you one or two we can consider you approach."

Her phone never rang.

Her door never opened.

She felt anything but free.

She read useless dossiers on uninspired targets. Rotated the vase of beach glass after closing each folder to catch the sun off the turn of the planet and spray its colored light across her sterile walls. She never reached into her bottom drawer—but only made the decision because of a powerful urge to reach—

The cool glass of the bottle; the flame of the gin burning my virgin throat

—and she spent those partial-duty hours obsessing on how she would use her new position to reacquire KALEIDOSCOPE.

Third week of September, vocal cords pronounced healed by Dr. Goldfarb, Lynn startled everyone to discover her voice was not her voice. Would never be the voice it was.

"Aunt Linny!" Charlotte chimed. "You sound like the lady who does Jessica Rabbit!"

"Better than the other dumb bunny. Oh, and thanks, Melody, for the stay—" and she announced to the family she found no reason not to move home.

"The summer was extra nice having you here." Melody squeezed both of her hands.

Love passed from Melody like a shock of dry lightning, and Lynn had an absurd thought.

She's terrified. Not by my leaving.

What is it?

Quizzical, probing, Lynn's expression only garnered Melody's smile. The affection glistening in her sister-in-law's eyes belied Lynn's concern; hot as the idea had burned into Lynn's consciousness, it extinguished in her mind without a trace of smoke.

Lynn breathed.

Autumn breathed.

Foxtail Farm breathed. The air of the living inhaled from the exhalations of all who came before. Who lived, who died, who walked the rooms, the corridors whose expirations remained to mix in the mingled and crisping air. Each breath of each living thing recycled from the breath of others present, or from the breath they left behind, like the turn of a kaleidoscope: fractured bits of sea glass, secret triumphs and torments, and lost love despairs.

September flamed out in a desperate heatwave. The sap in the trees in and around Foxtail Farm boiled and split trunks. No one bothered—because no one knew—to look for the devil's face, grinning in the seams as, summer spent, his day swiftly approached.

♛ ♛ ♛

First Monday of October. Lynn awoke alone in her Rock Creek Terrace condominium. Alone in her bed. Alone, she finished the water she'd left on the night-stand. Alone in spirit, neither happy nor appreciably sad. Noticed the tablet she used all summer to communicate coated with a light layer of dust.

Good and goodbye.

Funny, when forced to write every word you would otherwise automatically say, the amount of Lynn's language that came out as lies was garish. Words themselves, now unneeded of individual/selective focus, the gut wrench that went along with the observation lost its obtrusive luster. She opened the draperies. The day bright. Wisps of high clouds brushed the blue with white horsetails.

Speech improved cover.

She touched glass.

Colder today.

Somehow led to—

"'Bout time for some proper work." Aloud and husky. "Alone."

Eh. Good God.
Sultry.

♕ ♕ ♕

NATIONAL RESOURCES, for as long as it went back, was
the Agency stash for those the cut below the cut
above. Work-shy. Burnouts. Can't-miss-church/five of
seven/nine-to-fivers. The stash for the guys and gals
aces at the art of pitching a recruit—could teach it, some
did, at the Farm—but who pulled jokers in practical
foreign language aptitude. Couldn't pitch "live" to save
their lives out in a foreign field.

The FBI, who cried "foul" to have the CIA pitching agents on home turf, derided and abused them.
FBI domestic/CIA foreign. But the worst—the true dis-
dain reserved for NR operators—was held by officers of
the Clandestine Service who made their bones busting
bones in dirty, blazing-hot/freezing-ass hostile territory.

Foreign fields. Might take a month of dead-dropped
coded messages to arrange a single meet. A week or two
more of dry SDR runs, before a green-light go-order,
a precisely timed no-turning-back freedom/capture,
life/death run into hostile territory for a two-minute
contact in the foulest corner of a nasty city. Or the length
of a block in a hop-in/hop-out, hip-hop blaring/voice
disguising car ride. Or a heart attack safe house.
Where concentration double-duties calming/question-
ing/hearing your agent while the whole-time dialing-in,

twice alert, to the sound—or the dead silent lack of it—of a security service surrounding.

The pitch to the NR asset that Michael—

Scissors. Jousting knights.

The red balloon.

Oh, where are you? What's happened?

Push it out. Away and gone, balloon to the sky. Not now. Pointless wallow in hell.

—Michael called it the *"Hey, want a run at the headquarters gift shop?"/"Let's grab some tacos and beer,"* open-line call to the Dudley Do-Rights or Bond-cosplay-fantasists who recently got a lucky break from Exxon/GE/Microsoft/Goldman Sachs and were transferring, first-class abroad, civilian-patriots who wouldn't mind *"keeping a sharp eye out."* Ever easier, the American NR asset corporate-rotated home.

"So, who'd you meet? What'd you see? Whadja hear?" insistent tug at the sleeve as they're walking across the Mall.

Most NR recruits delivered jack shit; made recruitment in NR a numbers game. Though less prevalent—highly less successful—it went the same way with the Foreign Resources offshoot of NR who would attempt the same lame magic.

"Because work's too hard for numbnuts," so sayeth Michael

—on foreigners here at home. Scientists, students, journalists. The rare diplomat. Main problem? Target nations rarely send sleazeballs; those willing to sell out their country—after working so hard to prove themselves worthy of being sent in the first place—those were golden horn unicorns. But—and here was the worst of it—with the influx of cash and employment expansion brought by 9/11, the subsequent tidal wave of less than optimum recruits making it into the Agency to fill new slots, Director Tenet mandated foreign resource agents build out to parity with the CIA's NR American sources.

The stack of "potentials" on Lynn's desk rose from patty-pat sandcastle-size to a daunting ziggurat wall. Sand as well. All of them.

But it was October. It was cool. Finally. Lynn could breathe, and she would not let Silas—because, now back in business, that's who put her here—get her to bounce.

She cut a crenellation into the file-wall. Pulled a chunk of profile folders and went to work.

My unicorn's in here—somehow, somewhere. I swear to you, Michael, wherever you are, I'm going to find someone with a key to KALEIDOSCOPE. A name, a nationality, an organization will tumble and trip the bolt.

I will open the door. I will find you.

Eight struck-out days later. Headed to her Porsche. No bolts had popped. Like she told herself yesterday and the day before—

It'll happen tomorrow.

Engaged the engine. Flipped on NPR. Put it in reverse as the hypnotist-voiced journalist, reporting on the year-end international oil conference in Azerbaijan, let her know she'd already missed one man who, while he didn't hold the key, might get her close enough to the door for Lynn to pick the lock.

Who was that guy? Elmin something-or-other—the Azerbaijan embassy comms officer with the is-he-or-isn't-he bisexual secret? Married, but family permanently in Baku. Wife visits every few months. He flies the other way for holidays. Flies the other *way when she's not around and he heads to D.C.'s Kalorama district. Three/four times a year. Disappears into the Kalorama club scene. Nothing hard kink. No bathhouses. Huge precautions.*

Elim Hasanov—that's it. Kind of rhymes with Casanova. Easy.

Perfect personal opsec. Zero indication his own people have a clue. Foreign Resources bombed out already, taking runs at him. Men and women. Won't even engage in casual bar talk. Zero interest. A good-luck-with-that waste of effort.

Why Bitch-Boss allowed me his file.

But what about not *him? What about his car? His car guy. What was* his *name?*

Halfway out of her parking space, her thumbs drummed her steering wheel. Someone tooted/scooted around.

Sayadov. Aydin Sayadov.

Back in her spot. Back out of the Porsche, heels gun-shotting her back into the building.

Thirty-four. Born: Sumgait, Azerbaijan. Arrived, 2007. Work visa. Private luxury autos; three Mercedes to the embassy in 2010, two BMWs and an Audi to embassy staff last year.

Through security. Around the atrium. Elevators up. Details flooding back.

First sale: a Range Rover to good ol' Elmin. A good ol' deal. In return, Elim arranges all the others. Then,

January. Helps his boy Aydin push through his green card.

Unlocked her door. Straight to her desk. Back into the file stacks. No file on the car guy. Zero interest.

Hit him up?

Computer. Security fob. Log in. Search. SAYADOV, AYDIN...

Gay or not—don't care. Elmin has a thing for him, and suddenly I have a thing for Elmin.

Facebook profile. Posts: private. Friends private. Pics? Sexy cars. Sexy girls and cars. Sexy guys and cars. Champagne. Profile pic: lean, handsome—

I could go for those puppy dog eyes

—Lululemon tennis shirt and Fila shorts and a pose in front of the Rock Creek Tennis Club.

Time to dig up my racquet. Brush up my game. Five minutes—when he tells me what kind of a leg-up my Boxster trade-in will get—my legs and his pulse will tell me the kind of recruitment ahead of us.

3.

*I*T BEGINS, AND IT *ends. Every night unwinding, play and repeat. It begins, it ends, always the same way.*

Oscar Meyers blister on a coat hanger skewer. The sleeve of Pringles; crumbs on my fingertips. Sticky root beer jug. Dolley Madison Chocolate Zinger wrapper he throws into the fire. Watches it melt. Its stink masks the stink of his Mississippi beer and his glug-glug turpentine.

I roll over inside my Hello Kitty sleeping bag. Awakened by Mississippi Mud snores. Awakened by drizzle. By embers sizzling in the fire.

Extreme in close: the black hole of the pistol barrel. The cylinder behind it; nubs of five bullets and the sixth one, shell empty.

Happy big-girl eleven to me.

I point the gun at him. Boozy and snuffling, tangled in a painter's tarp. Both my thumbs strain on the ridged hammer. The last time I had the chance. Like then, now, like forever: the rough-metal-under-my-thumbs, straining to lever it back, lost moment forever captive to time.

Boone Kelso awakens at the hammer cock.

Do it right!

Like then, now, like forever. Play/repeat.

He fuddles conscious, confused, unsteady, furious. Bull bellows. Grabs the barrel with his hand in his shirtsleeve. I relinquish it. The only sound: hard breath—mine/his—and the fire's pop.

My father rustles a Ziploc baggie. Seals the pistol inside.

"Pray, child, on your mama's murdered soul, you never see this again. It'll be what hangs you."

But I'm not a child anymore. Not his child. I'm me now. My own children.

I stare at my all-grown hand. No matter how hard I shake it, no matter how violently I fling/I flick my wrist, I cannot throw my cell phone from my palm and Boone Kelso's face—

(You are not my father. You cannot be my father anymore.)

—his face leers at me, thrusting outward between flaming jail bars. A snarling, snapping dog. Hellfire (my childhood home, "Hellfire," he calls it) blazing behind his thick, untamed mane of hair, black as depthless infinity. My mother's corpse crisped inside.

He breathes. The cellphone breathes.

A serpent's tongue uncoils and wags inside his open mouth. Words roar from his throat: "Coming, child. Coming soon for you. Soon for them. Better find my be-all/end-all-American-dream-damnation."

To hell I will.

Melody's eyes snap open. Every night, since Paige's birthday, in orange luminescence, the clock displays 4:12 or 4:13 or 4:15, never 4:14. And Melody gathers the bedsheet. Pulls it. Smooths it over her. Over Hal, in the darkness, horizontal beside. Each early morning black, Melody steadies her breath by matching it to his. She breathes in his love and breathes out her hate. She waits until she can believe she hears all of Foxtail Farm inhaling/exhaling, love in/hate out. The children, adults, the chimneys, the walls, the spaces between, and dawn twilight creeps, gray inside like mice with mouse-work set to do.

Melody rise-and-shine. Briefly joining Doris, their pair fills the mirrors filling the house—Doris forever poised in burst-forth attitude, Melody to mouse-work of her own.

Each morning, she made her way to the kitchen. Made the coffee alone. Set it to its drip-drop-dribbling, before she walked onto the east porch and trimmed the white slats of the plantation shutters (all except the pair left dark above poor Gwen) to catch first light when it arrived at an angle just right.

Let light slide gently inside without glare. Without surprise.

Hal would be awake now—shower, shave, watch, wallet, keys, gun—before swinging through the kitchen for his thermos. Out-the-door-early to the temp duty he'd been shuffled. Post-Syria/post-Turkey/post- the "never happened" seven-days-gone he took at Paige's birthday.

Melody wasn't fearful for him; whenever Hal rode out to meet life-and-death stakes, Melody never experienced anxiety in the slightest. But home, Hal was desperate she ask him, desperate to tell her but knowing he would not—security and his personal code to bear—and, as she would never come between Hal and his faith, Melody simply watched his quiet, unyielding torment smolder beneath the gray ash of Kingston summer.

At least Quantico was a name he could say aloud. "Range instructor" was a title that went with a job he could mention. The twins liked having their daddy around that whole, hot summer's length. Although Hal was deeply adrift within himself, outwardly to Jack and Little Silas, he was a rock solid Funtown. They rode his back. Hung off his arms and on his legs, each boy a clinging moccasin to his bare feet as he carried them down the weathered stairs to the beach. They could "Hop on Pop" like their Dr. Seuss book. Airplane ride his feet extended over his head until he catapulted them from the wet sand into the water where they howled and shook their shaggy hair and clambered out and back over him. Their personal amusement park of Daddy fun-o-rama.

My sweet, strong Hal. Home from wherever Lynn sent you; argued about the two of you, and barely spoken to each other since. My heart-strong/heart-broke man: a second time returned without Michael, your beloved brother—I know that's where you went, wherever it was—and I watch you aching when you think I'm not looking. You hold your pain outside my reach.

After Melody made her morning rounds opening the house, she would pour his coffee and she would close his fist around his thermos as he would inevitably whisper—

"Don't ask me to tell you."

It so doesn't help he can't make love to me.

"I would never. I haven't."

He'd stare into her eyes. She would stare back into him. And she would say, as matter-of-fact—

"Right now, being our sons' daddy is a safe place—and that's you loving the best of all who I am. Take your space. Take your time. I'm here, and I'm there inside-a'them and, truly, honey, I *am* happy for you—because," she smirked, "I can't take the bear-cub climbing like you can. Here's your coffee. Get outta here."

"I love you, Melody Kingston."

"Good. Means the hex I put on you still's working."

Hal would leave.

Melody would fill her mug. Would creep through the French doors back onto the east porch. Ever-mouse-quietly, she would open the creaky screen door. Did this each morning. Slide the hold-open washer along the bar for Gwen, who, soon awake and fooling no one, tiptoed outside and drove away as if she'd not slept over.

Melody would sit on the steps. Watch night succumb to morning. Watch gray fill with air to balloon across the lawn and rise the walls of the North Vista Outhouse, and further out, expand over the catty-corner chapel drawing gold upward beneath it from the dew-dropped tips over every grass blade until summer dawn burst night gone.

God, thank you for letting me wake to another day.

She'd "Cheers" the holiness with her mug and rise with a smile and finish, every day that summer, with—

Protect Michael and bring him safely to the peace he seeks. And if it favors you, it'd be a good favor to Hal and the rest of us: let Michael's peace be home.

She would hear the elongated chittering sound she awaited. The chitter followed by a high, rough and insistent scream, strangely like radio static, and Melody would walk toward the abandoned tobacco fields and toward its source.

⚜ ⚜ ⚜

MICHAEL WAS GONE—to parts/fate-life-death unknown—so his family remained at Foxtail Farm the entire summer. Charlotte and Leigh shared the old playroom their dad, Uncle Hal, and Aunt Linny played in as children; Melody gave Paige one of the guest rooms. A guest room that in Silas's generation had never known a guest.

The graduation ceremony for Pancras Hall seniors had taken place at the end of May; Paige, capped-and-gowned and clutching a sprig of hawthorn blossoms that symbolized protection and hope, but to which Silas jabbed, "They print that in the pamphlet, and it's cute. But the true meaning of hawthorn carried by a young woman—back to when time began—is to protect her fertility from witches. So watch out."

Paige swatted him with the sprig. "The reason some of us get to carry the hawthorn isn't witches, it's the Piscataway. They used hawthorn as the primary ingredient in their medicines."

"And a hawthorn tomahawk gets you a what?"

"It gets me out of undergraduate biology, chemistry, and anatomy—the college classes I took to get the—" a silly change in tone— "Honor of the Carrying Branch."

Silas puffed, proud. "I'm glad the *Operation* game I gave you paid off."

Paige grinned. "Yeah, but—" a wiggle of blossoms— "it's also why I still owe fifty course-hours this summer."

"And college? Pre-med?"

Sheepish, she blushed, sheepish she shrugged. Then Clive came along to fleece her of her heart and pre-med was shut-the-door back to bed whenever she was home.

After the terrible night of her birthday, Paige burned through summer at Foxtail Farm as unfamiliar and dispassionate as a boarder, coming and going in the completion of her classes but participating in nothing else. Didn't take a summer job. Had planned for a gap year, but planned no travel, and the romantic summer fling she (and all of them, except maybe Silas) had expected would make her magical memories of that "Eighteen Summer" you only get once, had disastrously flung. Flung in her face. She went around with a burned-edged paper-mask smile hung on a storm cloud of inaccessible solitude.

♛ ♛ ♛

MELODY APPRECIATED Paige much more than Gwen, her unmotherly mother, to whom Melody had also offered a bedroom, but who refused her offer out of anger and resentment for Silas.

"The girls can stay, but I will drive home nights and sleep in my marriage bed. Empty though it is! And pray you get-this-right—Silas! Lynn! —and you stop lying, Hal, you dick! —and you spy-people—" Madwoman/money-getting-tight, liquor making her tighter—hair tearing shriek: "Fucking get Michael home or give me my fucking money!"

Gwen inevitably and woefully would linger too long with the box of wine. Too long with the girls at TV, or with the twins at Chutes and Ladders. Too-long with the soft/scratchy throw blankets on the "back row" sofa, close to the wet bar, and Melody thought Paige was something remarkable, every night sneaking down to clean up Gwen's Kleenex box. To throw out her wet, wadded tissues. Rinse her sticky wine glass even as she muttered (the same, each night, all fervid summer long) "You really suck, Mom," before tucking Gwen in—drunk out, cried out—on the sofa where, knocked out, Gwen slept.

Poor Gwen.

Gwen. Who made such a ghastly, ugly pass at Clive Lancer, who crushed her daughter's heart.

The rest of the family—from Melody and Hal's twins who at age six intuited it, to Silas who vociferously urged it on—waited through August and into the dead slack of September for the two of them—un-mother and board-er-daughter—to finally out with their knives and have at the fight.

♕ ♕ ♕

THE THIRD DAY of the new month was Labor Day. Hal and Gwen, holiday off, Lynn dropped in before break-fast: all of them together, their differences for that day, put aside. The unspoken torment of Michael's birthday without him came heavily upon the Kingstons. No one looked forward to the day ahead. Then Leigh brought the family an unexpected flash of brightness. She came downstairs wearing her Paul Revere costume. Captivated them all.

"Listen, my children, and you shall hear / Of the midnight ride of Paul Revere, / On the eighteenth of April, in Seventy-Five: / Hardly a man is now alive / Who remembers that famous day and year."

A deep breath—and they all drew a sigh of relief along with her, exhaled with hope and a tender unity—she continued.

"He said to his friend, 'If the British march / By land or sea from the town to-night, / Hang a lantern aloft in the belfry-arch / Of the North-Church-tower, as a signal-light,— / One if by land, and two if by sea; / And I on the opposite shore will be, / Ready to ride and spread the alarm / Through every Middlesex village and farm, / For the country-folk to be up and to arm.'"

Lynn spontaneously held out her open arms. With the meeting of their eyes, the pull of nature moved Leigh's first step to her biological mother, but—

"Oh. My. God!" Gwen shouted, freezing Leigh in her tracks. "You are my smartest little bean. I swear you are."

Leigh dutifully hugged her mother first.

Lynn made a quick knuckle-brush beneath her eye. Hers were not the only eyes with tears. Tears each one of them had expected to shed that miserable day, over Michael's void that haunted them, flowed softly with joy and pride. Each, in their own special way, remembered what it was to love their country, and reminded themselves, the sacrifices they made to keeping it, and that convinced them—each one in their heart—that Michael was acting—wherever he was, whatever he was doing—in compact to that ideal.

"Dad's crying!" Jack laughed.

"You guys are silly," said Little Silas, but unlike his brother, he didn't feel like laughing.

"Correct, my lambs—Dragoons *never* cry. Leigh? Get your reward," said Silas, the half of the fifty-dollar bill he had torn for her already in his hand. This morning moment, anticipated by the old spook.

Leigh scrambled up the stairs—They all heard her squeal of, "Didja like it, Gramma Doris?"—and trampled back, holding the other half.

True to his words, Silas fused the currency together, a bit of OTS science that seemed a lot like wizardry.

♔♔♔

IT WAS A SECRET. Not that Melody was keeping it from anyone—

Not like my nightmare: all too real, too soon here...

Nothing like that. But all the same, something no one knew about. A gentle thing she didn't share with anyone. She stumbled upon it in June and returned each morning since. Closer and closer, until now she was accepted as part of this new-and-'nother family.

Melody walked out from the field path among the sheds and old structures. Through dead weeds and the dust. Past the old slave quarters where only hard-packed dirt depressions remained of where their cabins once stood, and as she came around that ghostly place, past the drying shed, she called, "Good morning, Beyonce!"

The fluffed and eager barn owl who paced the jutting, gray-ancient beam outside her hollow-hole, long lanky legs of white downy bloomers—deliberate runway couture attitude—stopped.

"Jay-Z still out?"

The owl turned her heart-shaped face and blinked at Melody—sometimes it beak-clacked a "mind-your-own"—but Jay-Z, on broad wings with talon-dangled prize, would choose the moment of Melody's arrival to swoop with a roar of wind over Melody's head.

Laughing and holding her hair, Melody ducked. Jay-Z gave a boastful scream to his mate, and Melody smiled at the miracle of the world—sunrise-tipped and glimmered—as the mother owl she called Beyonce, tore apart the field mice for the pair's owlets purring and cooing inside their hole.

Melody had no way of knowing how the owls' blood spoke to them. That they were descendants of those bedeviled raptors once scorned and stoned by slave and Kingston boys that hellish summer three centuries past.

She left the owls to their breakfast. Ducked inside the old ruin. Took the letter, hidden in her pocket, and read it again. Alabama Post-Prison Parole Board. Her father, Boone Kelso, qualified for halfway house early release. She shoved it into a hollow hole of her own where it nested beside another letter. From Richmond DA, Calvin Kirby. One of a dozen begging Melody to break her silence; to give testimony against her father in the unsolved murder of Roberta Kelso.

Her mother.

Who she shot dead.

Nights lingered longer.

Coffee steamed harder in the cooler air of dawn, and by October, Melody walked mornings in darkness. The brood of owlets grown from nestlings to fledglings to juveniles practiced roosting outside the drying shed. Surrounded Melody—mouse-work complete—in trees, and on other structures, on top of old telephone/electrical posts, wires long detached and gone, white-faced, gold-glittering-eyed like swivel-headed judges. Melody spooked. This was the morning of the night where it all came to a head over the dinner she made to celebrate the end of Paige's final forty-five-day high school sprint out of Pancras Hall for good. It was the week before Halloween.

❧❧❧

MORGAN EIGER, Paige's best friend and—that summer, like the summer before, and conceivably the next and the next beyond that—Hollywood Township's worst-intentioned seductress was taking a tear through male hearts aged fourteen to twenty-four. Like an Indian counting coup and taking scalps. Morgan had finished, in that lively eyed way of hers, the telling of a story that somehow grew those eyes wider until the turquoise in them gleamed and mesmerized like chrome. She had Charlotte, Leigh, and the twins, edge of their seats, mouths agape, the adults leaning back and slyly grinning, as she concluded, "Bobby Claypoole and I dug up that 'Here-kitty-kitty' cat. That White House kitty-cat, Socks. And just like predicted: all that was left was fur and leather and bone."

"Did it still have its socks feet?" Jack.

"The fur sorta indicated. You bet."

"Did you bring her the skull?" Charlotte. "The First Lady, like she sent you?"

"I did. I brought Ms. Hilary that Sock's skull, and now when she wants to spy on her Bill, she peers through its empty sockets and she can see through his old cat's eyes what it is the old Mr. President is up to."

Without missing a beat, Morgan swiveled in her chair, aiming her silver-blue gaze disconcertingly at Paige's eyes. "And if *you'd* had the skull of my old cat, you'd have seen me looking at Clive back two nights after your birthday."

Now? From months ago?

"What?"

"In Old Town. Getting a last turtle mud cup with sprinkles before leaving, and you'd've heard him saying—" sing-song— "*he sti-ill loves you.*"

Paige didn't respond. Everyone stared, waiting for her to say something, and it became apparent the grandfather clock in the front hall wouldn't tick until she did. In that pendulum frozen second, flooded with memory and emotion and a penetrating thought that the only thing that made them best friends was they'd been thrown together in the pre-K nursery at St. Pancras Hall, a place they were now finally free from—so *that* didn't have to hold them to anything like loyalty/friendship/let-alone-love— "Morgan: You're a bitch."

Morgan, running the same train of thoughts the other direction back to station, gently stroked Paige's forearm. "Only because I attached it to a ghost story, but it was honest to goodness, the truth." The chrome melted; the turquoise glistened wet. "I didn't know any way to get it out and tell you—all summer—so you'd really hear. I've been dying to. Bitch that I am. You know that."

Paige looked at Morgan's hand still on top of her arm like she was stroking poor dead Socks, and Paige sparked alive.

She said, "'Still?' He said, 'still loves me?' He *loved* me? He *does*?!"

"His words. Not mine!" And they were interlacing their hands, and Gwen, waiting those same months for an opening—

"Oh! If I could take *anything* back this summer—"

Paige snapped eyes. Burning. Spiteful. "Stop it. If the next word out of your mouth isn't *Dad*, as in *If I could take anything back this summer, it would be divorcing Dad*—"

Gwen, undeterred, wanting so much to get something from this conversation for herself— "If you hadn't of flown out like a banshee, you'd have seen—"

"Shut up, Mom. I saw him kissing you."

"I was kissing *him*. You may think I'm just your mother, but I am a very attractive—extra-ordi-*very*-nary seductive woman."

"And you're gross as shit, so shut up."

"That'll do, Paige." Silas.

More silence. The Kingston kind that burned.

Ever since Melody pointed it out, Hal didn't much like the way his twins stared at their aunt; the way she posed—especially when using words like *attractive* and *seductive*. "Boys—and girls, if you guys want—let's go to the kitchen and start on the pumpkins."

"Those won't be ready until tomorrow," Melody said. "They carve best a couple days off the vine."

And Silas, again: "Hal, you and the boys sit. Girls have already figured it out, but the twins need the whole lesson from Auntie Gwen."

"What're you talking about?" Gwen-snap-Silas.

"Keeping your boobs in your shirt in front of my sons!" Hal-snap-Gwen.

"Melody's always shoving hers in their face!" Gwen-snap-Melody, who busted out laughing.

"They are my sons. I can hug them to my chest whenever I want, and you have very prominent bosoms yourself and they are *attractive* and *seductive* and, you know it's perfectly natural—Jackie, Little Silas—to look. To look. It's perfectly normal. And—" softly, simmering, though gentle— "Hal, I shouldn't have made a deal out of it."

Gwen kind of tucked herself into her chair. Wondered—only an errant wonder—if her curls still held. "My point is Clive was telling me 'No,' and pushing me away. That's the truth, Paige. And it's all I want to say on the subject."

Paige knew it wasn't. Melody knew it wasn't. Lynn—if she'd been there, knew it wasn't.

Silas looked at Paige. They shared a secret about Clive. So, it's possible anything he might have said next would throw her off as much as these words did: "I, for one, wish he would come back. You two made a fine pair. Never know. Still might."

"Papa, how could I ever forgive him?"

"Those with the most virtue suffer the most from the plague of temptations."

Gwen didn't need to speak. If she wasn't exactly on the right track, at least she was off the dead-end lane with the potholes and caltrops. But this was Silas. And his was a pronouncement. And she'd slept over three months on the old bastard's sofa and was no closer to figuring out how to get hold of Michael's pay that kept coming in *to him* (instead of her, who deserved it), and she'd gotten some kind of chlamydia or something that didn't show symptoms by one of the gay guy's she'd bopped around with, had passed her a prescription his doctor said *she* needed to take, and it was all so humiliating (especially because it was private and she couldn't cry over it to any effect), and—this bore repeating—*this* was Silas.

Asshole father-in-law.

To Gwen's detriment, she spoke. "Fix it all with one of your silly quotes from your King Arthur book."

Silas folded his hands. Silas leaned in. "Beg your pardon, dear?"

"Oh. What? Not King Arthur? The Bible?" Now she glanced around for allies. "*Is* it from the Bible?"

"Nothing so weighty," Silas purred.

Gwen brightened enough to cackle. "Well, what? Where'd you dredge your little wisdom-citisism from?"

He tapped his chest. Pointed out his heart. Three times hard. But his gaze locked with Paige's.

He wants me to know he means it for me. Those with the most virtue suffer the most from the plague of temptations.

Because they had a secret about Clive. A secret which, sort of explicitly, marked Silas a murderer— Silas's words suddenly seemed to mark that as true.

"Try speaking from it, Gwen. Your heart. It'll do wonders for you better than the doxycycline you've been popping with your coffee—whatever that's for/none of my business—on the way to your car, sneaking out each morning like a wannabe thief." He rubbed his hands together. He hadn't gotten her there yet. "What did you catch, if you don't mind telling?"

That did it. Flood of tears. Gwen stormed out. Melody gave an exasperated huff at Silas. "*Every* time?"

"I don't like crybabies."

Paige was pleased as punch, but Leigh burst into tears, and Silas's hands—bridged so confidently on the table over his plate—collapsed with sudden dishonor.

Morgan whispered, "I'm gonna go. He does love you, by-the-way, and maybe he is—Your grampa's a dick, no offense, Mr. Kingston—"

"None taken, potty-mouth."

"But he's always right—maybe Clive is coming back."

Paige stood with her. Clutched and "Bye'd." Loved her best friend.

Melody changed her mind on the whole carving fresh-plucked pumpkins idea. Headed her team and Charlotte, comforting Leigh, to the kitchen. Except for Paige and Silas, the room was empty.

Paige walked around Doris's round table to where her grandfather remained in his chair.

He said, "I messed up." Gloomy-eyed her. "I'd never do anything to hurt your sister. She has so much already ahead of her."

"Mom brings out the worst in us." She wrapped her arms around his bullet head. Pulled it into his chest. Kissed his crown.

The house took a breath, and the wind moaned through the chimney of the common room fireplace.

"You hear her?"

"I always hear her, Papa."

Silas rose. Looked upon his eldest grandchild. "Do me a favor."

"What?"

Fall wind rattled screens. The shutters. The house respired in a sound like faraway female merriment. Paige yelp-laughed. Showed Silas her arm: the goosebumps. The standing hair.

"Doris can do that," he chuckled. "All I was going to say is—before *you* interrupted us—" Doris/the house— "is don't trust everything she tells you. The horse Doris still rides in this race, I'm afraid, comes straight from hell."

His words did nothing to soften the hair bristling Paige's arm; she watched him blow a kiss at a mirror—a convex glass mirror—beside the French doors. And the way the image of her grandmother bent in the glass, Doris didn't appear so much as lunging out, but lunging directly at Paige to drag her in.

Paige hurried past it to the warm safety of Melody's kitchen, the holiday smell of pumpkin guts already wafting, and remembered how Dad taught her the French name those curved mirrors came with.

From the Middle Ages.

Oeil de sorcière.

The Witch's Eye.

Paige shuddered and, like everyone everywhere does, pretended ghosts can't hurt the living because ghosts aren't real.

<h1 style="text-align:center">4.</h1>

S TARS GONE. SKY GONE. No drift. No lap at the hull. No breeze. No empty air. All gone. The fog complete. Lake Geneva, gone within it. Michael Kingston, in soul, spirit, capacity for thought, not far behind.

He held the dead woman's face. His thumbs wiped tears—his own—splattered upon her cool, soft cheeks. There were muscles beneath the skin. Muscles built from years of happiness. Smiles wide and often. If she had been told in life she would end this night shot dead by someone working for the Chinese, a paper stuffed in her mouth with the Chinese morpheme symbols that represented the word *Kaleidoscope*, she would never have believed it. But if someone had forced the truth upon her in such a way as she must, Helene Favre might have smiled then, a little, too. Astonishment could always bring a devilish grin to her face.

Of Helene's hair, Michael had only seen it coiled, piled, pinned into a soaring trestle, but in the struggle of her murder, the explosive force of the close-range bullet strike that finished her, her hair collapsed. It surrounded and cushioned her head in a blanket of fine gray and white silk, and the fog, finer than any silk, wove her plaits and veiled her face, thickened around her as though enswathing her in a cocoon.

Stars gone, sky gone, gone most of all, Mrs. Helene Favre. Dead on the *Échalote* foredeck.

Michael stumbled up. Stumbled back. The fog clung. Wouldn't release him. It climbed him and it smothered. Inhaled through his nostrils, he felt the fog inside his head, encouraging the metamorphosing of his mind away from his personality, the purpose that held him to the how. And the why. The who and the what he was of himself.

My "all" gone too. Only choice: to fog all choice.

His feet. Stumbling, hunting.

Ladder down.

Ducking. Stumbling. Hunting. Hands.

Twist the Kingston valves. How's that for confession?

Sea cocks—otherwise known as Kingston valves—opened. Flood the ballast tanks. Ballast cover plates removed. Overflow and flood the barge.

His decision to take the black inflatable dinghy, decision to abandon Helene, to abandon the *Échalote*, abandon the lake, Switzerland, his past/present/future, the CIA, his decision to abandon the secret picture at the bottom of the kaleidoscope of his life: Michael took the decision that he might abandon the man he'd culminated into and must now escape.

Michael lowered the rubber boat. Lowered into it. Locked the oars. He dipped the blades. He paddled from the flooding craft. Sensible enough to know he fled a murder scene, the swath of crimes that led to it, his behavior was not precipitated by any desire to evade justice. To elude the law. To avoid the consequences of his life and his choices. His behavior, this July night, was Michael eschewing life itself. With the death of Helene Favre, something snapped inside of Michael Kingston. A switch—inside his head—flipped with Helene's murder; switch broken, mind broken, his heart. A switch that ordered his soul to manifest death as existence. His body to pass through life as a ghost of flesh and blood.

He breathed fog and he pulled the oars, roiling it. He pictured the dark water rising around Helene's corpse. The line rising to her cheek. Over her eyes. The tip of her nose. Her hair spreading, blooming, water lily white. It was better for his brain and the tasks ahead to picture this than see her as the fog-figure hunched and huddled in the dinghy's prow who wouldn't lift her head to face him and, as it might be a fog-cast Helene, it might as easily be Gwen or Lynn or Doris.

Paige, Charlotte, or Leigh.

Forget me.

Helene showed qualities missing from the other two significant women in his life—Doris and Gwen. She did not love him in any way comparable to mother or wife. And yet, not being tied to him biologically or by marriage contract/societal convention, this only magnified the love Helene expressed. Treated him with more faith and commitment.

The nose of the black rubber boat ground over rocky sand beneath a knee-high grassy verge. Fog swirled over it. Michael carried himself along, passing through a clump of trees onto the corner of a switchback road. A sign indicated that to continue would take him to the monastery-castle, the Château de Ripaille.

France. Move. Walking. Away from the castle. A road through a forest. Into the foggy ditch beside the road. His hand found the gun in his waistband. Broken to pieces, he tossed it into morning darkness among the trees and shrubs he passed.

Breast pocket. Pinwheel's cigarette pack. Handwriting inside the lid. An address. Meant nothing to him; wouldn't allow it to mean more. Michael crumpled the pack. Tossed it. No less than six borders between here and there, he walked in the opposite direction.

Any moment, a passing vehicle might be police. Might notice him. Might stop him, take him in, and the difficulties that would follow would be mighty. The logical part of Michael's brain accepted this probable/looming fate, but it no longer triggered his fight/flight mechanism. He simply ambled on.

A service station convenience store. Some chips. Late breakfast/early lunch. A television behind the cashier. The *Échalote* police/rescue/salvage boats. Helene's photo—from the opening of her Laundrenet. Happy years ago.

He loved her face. Saw it in the woman beside him. Saw Helene beside him.

More video. Police tape and blockade around the shop. Around her apartment.

Body bag loaded into an ambulance.

Michael shut his eyes. When he opened them, he was rolling through farmland inside a commuter train. He blinked his eyes, and two days later, Michael saw his own face—vaguely recognizable from a traffic camera still-capture, better as a police sketch side-by-side—broadcast from another television, this one through the back kitchen door of a restaurant in Lyon's 3rd arrondissement. *Le Menekşe Derviş,* The Violet Dervish. Cupped fingers scooped oily clumps of spiced chicken, chickpea, baldo rice from a to-go carton while the *sans-papiers* Turkish dishwasher made calls about trading a diamond ring and a Canadian passport for cash. A new identity.

Ripped off on the diamond but taken care of with a reconditioned US passport, when finally recognized as the man wanted in connection with the murder of Helene Favre, it was four days, maybe a week, and he, in a railyard in Paris, getting mugged.

Money gone. Passport gone. Secondhand leather jacket and badass motorcycle boots he can't remember ever getting—gone. And the next to go: his life. The beat-down didn't stop, and—

Freeze frame: French words. Recognizing me. A fatal pause.

Hand-rock. Head-blood. The other guy. Face: blood.

Money, passport, jacket, boots—ah, yes! Church thrift sale; Dijon last week—not gone/mine.

His beard came. Filled out. His look, homeless. His look deranged. Always the hoodie from under the leather. Always eating at kitchen doors or bins. Avoiding daylight. Avoiding street cameras. Avoiding his picture, which was everywhere until—

I'm vanished. It's gone.

Ignored in a routine police check on a train—bypassed Brussels—arrived Antwerp; instead of interrogation, told where to go for a shower and a bed. Warned of the penalties for vagrancy.

Michael blinks. He's in August walking into September and anything written is in German, like everything heard, and days pass surrounding him with cities of quivering heat, heat that rises from sidewalks to blend into leering faces carrying on life among one another but never with him. Days pass where he doesn't speak more than a sentence or two, regardless of how often he's spoken at from faces that leer or sneer. That blend. That peer/soothe/curse and melt one into the other with the heat like the ice cream he's dropped and watches melt for an afternoon, melting on the sidewalk, while lava flows of people swirl—either side in both directions. Colors mix. Colors melt, harden, then its night (which is when Helene faithfully joins him to lead him onward, because without her, he has forgotten to move.)

"You are running at something at the same time you are running away from it."

The countryside is easier for Michael. Here, when they speak Polish, there was the Michael Kinston who could say in that language he doesn't speak a word of it, but rarely says a thing. Offers them a distracted listening to, if only to discern how far away from him he can make their voices blow—puffing his grizzled cheeks and spouting rancid air—when face to face he drives away life.

There was the other Michael Kingston who finds himself walking in place, making no discernible forward motion, who wouldn't pause at the rustle of cloth beside him; wouldn't flinch at the touch of fingers, hard, as binding wires and Helene would urge him trembling onward and the cities and towns would tumble behind him in crossword puzzles of mixed up names: Hanover,

Leipzig, Prague, Vienna, Krakow. Berlin. Krakow, again. And it's Doris on his other side, concentration camp Doris as she appeared that last horrible year of her poisoned life. Before she vanished.

"To my Michael: for your loyalty."

Berlin, again. Lviv—

His Russian ranked Level 3 on the Interagency Language Roundtable, he understands: *"My vybrasyvayem cherstvyy khleb v pyat'. We throw out the stale bread at five.* And he stands for hours that pass for days, and days that pass for minutes and the bread is placed in his hand everywhere he goes, or he's shooed off with the stray dogs.

And the insects.

Brest. Voices, insects, traffic, melting face, insects—

(Michael couldn't deny the insects any longer, not after Brest; one thousand insects follow in his wake.)

Insects, music and laughter, the clinking of dishes. The sound of September sudden rains followed by October brutal thunder. By golden sunfire leaf-burning brilliance, and trees and fields.

Always the insects.

He, the Pied Piper of insects no one else saw (or if they did, pretended) swarming behind him. Green, gray, brown, yellow and soft or brittle and in between and inside his clothing in a crawling, writhing-legged, buzzing, growing wave.

Sawing, sawing, legs and wings: he heard them sawing through the sides of trains. The windows. He watched fields and rivers and forests and towns and cities unrolling scroll-like and swarmed before his eyes and walking and followed by this enveloping mandibled and stinger'd pestilent multitude.

Minsk—

Helene's hand peels his black and curled fingers. "Have this water, friend. Drink. You'll die if you keep sitting here."

—and into Kyiv. The smell of subways, of libraries, piss, and of trains and traffic. He could hear the insects, breathing, millions of them now. Pulsing in the sewers and beneath the streets and inside the walls. He punctured towns like a hot needle through a blood blister, exploding out the other side of them in tumbling stolen rides on farm trucks. He is in Konotop. And he is in Kursk. And he is talking to Michael Kingston, the boy—swinging between Helene and Doris playing *"One, two, three: jump!"*

Am I back in Berlin?

Is this Paris?

Don't let this be There... Helene!

She holds him in an alley all night, stroking his matted hair and dirty bearded face, drug-addicted teenage girl who wears the melting faces of all three of his daughters, who whispers: *"You are running at something at the same time you are running away from it."*

The smell of earth and trees. Of sap. Blinks and stares at a fire. Briefly and brightly himself awakening with the last cry of help from his empty stomach. *If you don't eat, you will die.* Horror, confusion. A field where the grasshoppers descend. And he has laughed and chased them and trapped them with his t-shirt and stuffed them in a bag.

I'm doing this farmer a favor.

Taken to his fire. Cooked. Eaten. Hunger satisfied, Helene laid him to rest and when he awoke, time had lost its order. The hours jumbled, night and day became day within night-within-day; they conveyed no difference in his mind and bugs satisfy hunger.

The city doesn't matter. Never mattered. All bar windows look the same. And to Michael the cuckold, through the windows Gwen looks the same in every woman's clinch with every man, and sometimes women, through dirty glass; and he is Michael the professional liar posing as fake people to steal truth, and he is watching how *those* men might have lived if he had been the cover and Michael, ended, the legends had lived on.

Hard breathing. Hard running. The wind slapping his face, October half gone—hard-feet-hard-along a Tula sidewalk alongside a defunct locomotive factory. Horror in a face. Over a shoulder. Staring back. Running away: *"Otoydi ot menya, chertov bolvan!"*

In Tula, he's seen his father, Silas—impossibly younger than he ever knew him—and he chases him— "Silas! Dad!"

"Otoydi ot menya, chertov bolvan!" Get away from me, you fucking bum!

Michael arrested. Jailed. Hospitalized.

Michael forgotten.

Invisible to the suit-men, the nurses, the doctors, one day he walks across the yard and out the gate.

One morning, the morning he arrived, he wore the face of a scarecrow, the eyes of a drowned man. His beard was thick, though patchy in places where he'd shaved and forgotten to finish. One hundred days after Geneva. He buzzed the apartment. Stared into the camera lens. *"Ya prishel za mamoy. Ona zdes?" I've come for my mother. Is she here?* He collapsed on the doorstep.

An elderly man, goblin-like, plump, flabby-jowled, but with delicate hands attached to thin wrists. Goblin-man spoke to the doorman. Convinced him not to call the police. Reminded the doorman he was a doctor. Informed him this was his patient, and would he help carry Michael inside? He said this to Michael: *"Vas zhdali neskol'ko nedel' nazad." You were expected months ago.*

Michael smiled. Pinwheel's cigarette address.

Moscow.

The doorman pulled Michael to his feet. Braced him. With the doctor's help, they lugged him into an elevator. A red cushioned seat. The doorman set Michael down. Michael peered. Tried to make eyes grateful. The doorman offered his empty palm. The doctor filled it with folded currency. The man backed out. The elevator shut. The ill-made doctor focused on Michael in the mirror.

He spoke once more. *"Da. Tvoya mat' zhdet tebya v moikh komnatakh."*

Michael sobbed, and his tears washed the dirt from his cheeks. *Yes. Your mother is waiting for you inside my rooms.*

MICHAEL ONLY HAD A three-hour lead on the authorities between when he'd run aground on the French shore and when authorities boarded and secured the *Échalote*. The murder investigation opened. Within six hours, a vague full-figure image of the American pulled from street camera video matched to security video from the bar where Hal observed Michael entering Helene's storefront. Enhanced. A person of interest photograph distributed to the three Swiss police forces: communal, cantonal, and federal. Approved for media by 2 p.m. the first afternoon. By 5:00 p.m., fingerprints from the barge matched fingerprints from the Laundrenet. DNA would match.

Crime scene investigators processed Mrs. Favre's apartment as a second crime scene—assault/kidnapping/robbery. Insurance contacted. Jewelry or other valuables? A key to a safe deposit box discovered. A court order for the bank requested.

Meanwhile, a talented forensic artist with the canton police, working with digital investigators combing the city backward and forward in time from the two pieces of video evidence—Michael coming onto the street/Michael entering the Laundrenet—tracked

Michael in one direction: to the Coop Market coffee bar and a barista with a clear description. The other direction, to the Seespiegal restaurant. Linked to an unpaid bill. Another murder victim. Between the barista and the anti-smoking waiter, police artists rendered an exceptional sketch of Michael's face. Both witnesses corroborated the suspect's nationality as American.

The US Consulate General in Geneva, informed of the investigation, promised support. Assigned a consular attorney available for any needed oversight.

French authorities briefed. A liaison officer brought into the investigation. Interpol came next to coordinate the four remaining border states—Italy, Germany, Austria, and Liechtenstein—and to run the fingerprints through their Automatic Fingerprint Identification System (AFIS). A database with access to 196 member countries. A big fat zero. Due to the number of porous EU borders the suspect could access, they slapped a 24-hour rush on Michael's DNA material. The results, returned 48 hours later: no match.

This transpired within the hour of Michael's meal at *Le Menekşe Derviş*, walking distance from Interpol headquarters.

That same hour, the court granted an order for Helene Favre's bank that allowed Swiss Federal Police to seize Helene Favre's safe deposit box. An hour after that, contents removed and examined, everything changed.

Helene Favre's safe deposit box: Property deeds. Insurance policies. Her will. Her passport. Some jewelry. Some gold. A ribbon-tied set of love letters between Helene and her husband they had exchanged 1959-1962. Precious photographs of her childhood, of her parents, her grandparents, a tintype of their parents. And, at the bottom—because she had hoped it would never be the most desired item from a serene and joyful life—a pristine manila envelope with a letter.

Written the morning after Abbatantuono's suicide. Written in a labored and serious tone; spiderweb delicate and freely spun penmanship. A warning from beyond the grave. That she and the American "Joe"—she suspected was not a "Joe", and neither a cuckold of the suicide banker Abbatantuono, but some kind of American agent—might both be killed.

"If, however, I am killed, and he yet survives, in my injury and death, this man bears no guilt or responsibility or liability. All my acts and actions are taken of my free will without illusion or emotional distress or entanglement of persuasion. He is my friend."

The Swiss prosecutor assigned to the investigation hated the letter. Everything about it. Unless he produced physical evidence that directly linked their mysterious American Joe to the murder(s), or the letter was written under duress—though the flowery/overwritten language, the beautiful bespoke handwriting spoke to the opposite—he had no case against his prime suspect. That the letter had been witnessed, signed, and notarized by her longstanding family attorney, Helene Favre had gone far to provide a "get out of jail free" card for her American friend.

The mention of the Abbatantuono suicide gave the police another dead-end, movie star slammed-door-in-the-face, avenue of investigation as did—Day Four—the discovery of a middle-aged, end-stage emphysema emaciated Russian in a hotel room suicide.

A businessman of no particular business discovered by the maid service who had abided the *Do Not Disturb* lock-slot card until his check-out date came overdue. The man had cut his wrists in a wild self-struggle around the bedroom. The first wrist, high against the window. His other wrist dragging the bedclothes off the mattress—slice, slice, slice—entangling in them but only long enough to haul himself into the bathroom and throw himself into the tub where, pulling the curtain—ring-popping-ring-popping-ring—he slit his throat and ended it all. His passport was false. His fingerprints and DNA proved unrecorded.

Invited to the US Consulate, the lead Geneva local detective, the canton prosecutor, and the federal police detective coordinator raced each other there; each more eager than the other to hand over the case. Bow out. Tip their hats to the consul general. Withdraw from the room, wiping their feet and leaving it all on "American Soil."

The consul general handed it to the CIA Chief of Station, US Embassy Bern. The Chief of Station encoded/routed it to DDO Gary Gravin, who gave it to Harker, who slipped it under the table to Silas Kingston at the Department of Commerce, Office of Treaty Regulation and Administrative Compliance (OTRAC).

Pinwheel identified straight from the envelope. His killer, along with the unlucky fellow behind the restaurant, identified by Hal; more importantly, Hal's memory of these two matched the bit of Dulles surveillance footage of the non-SWAT/SWAT assassins of the TSA/not-TSA assassins back the night of July the Fourth.

Hal confirmed these men were American. They weren't working for Silas, CIA, FBI. And Kolya/Kalaydoskop wasn't about to cut off his own right hand. Left hand. Or throat.

Since Operation SIDESHOW, eleven years back—TIME MACHINE, ten—son of a bitch Nathan Muir's meddlesome antics with his clown show son and cast of derelict characters, including his own daughter Lynn, reared the head of the Chinese dragon. The dragon had been pushing the edges of KALEIDOSCOPE and growing bolder ever since. Silas had kept them in check. Assumed Kolya had on his end. But this was China, and China pushed inexorably.

Chess isn't Chinese Checkers. Chess is a two-opponent game. Europe learned the hard way, nations individually, together as a Union. They stopped pushing. Abdicated to the Atlanticist globalists and with them, there was too much greed and power for power's sake (which is spelled g-r-e-e-d), coupled with high-flying intellectualism and cunning brilliance for them to position themselves against KALEIDOSCOPE. (Spelled y-e-t.) But China would have to be watched. Messaged. Dealt with at an appropriate time...which appeared to be counting down to n-o-w "now."

Silas responded to Harker who kicked it to Gravin, who wrote it up for his CoS, who whispered into the Ambassador's ear, who made it clear to the Swiss their POI (aka American Joe, aka Arthur Danford, aka Michael Kingston) was to be left alone, avoided, and ignored. It would be best if they make the problem work out so that two suicides plus two murder victims equal a case-closed zero sum, game over.

Meryl Hofmyer said, "What do *we*, if-we-do—if there's something *to do*— Do about Michael-Arthur-America-Joe your—not to put too fine a point on it—firstborn? Would you like eyes on him, hmm?"

"No. That's been Lynn's mistake from the beginning. Her tugging from where she doesn't belong, Kalay-doskop tugging from the other end."

"I don't think it wise leaving Lynn inside the gate. Even kenneled where she can't do anyone any more damage. Because she can. Lynn Kingston, you-know-well-as-I *always* can. Will. Say the word, and I'll bounce her out on the under-the-influence workplace alcoholism of it all. She can get the help you know she needs."

"Aren't you sympathetic. Lift a finger against that girl—"

"No-need, no need to threaten. No need for fingers. But one day you will, mmm, recognize she's your Achille's heel."

Silas broiled her with a look.

"Where are we on Baku?"

"SIGINT up on every participant. Agents producing hardcopy. We have four electronic surveillance teams ready on rotation to rig the venue, put their special touch everywhere the attendees stay, go, or, eh, travel inside of."

"Once everyone arrives, I want constant eyes on them as well as audio. Everywhere."

"And, yes, mm-hmm, you shall have it. By the time the oil conference gavel-goes, we will already know everyone's endgame and beat them with our own. Which, however-though-you'd-know-it—" She gave him a placid look— "I am, detail-wise, behind on, ehn?"

Silas pretended her little chunter hadn't carried a question mark. He removed his sweater. Immediately cold. Forgotten how frigid they kept the air in this damned old Hoover Building; colder than old Herbert C. rotted in his grave.

"I'm going out."

"It is the first of October. The morning wasn't exactly hot, I expect—" checked her wristwatch— "after, say, one o'clock, it will creep down."

"Good for that. Got a jacket in the car. I won't be back. But if you get cold, crank the heat on our China assets. I want to know how far they've penetrated us and who the hell I don't know they have turns the wheel."

She gazed at her many years mentor with her bright, dead eyes. She always got the job he wanted done better than anyone who'd ever served beneath him, and many times more ruthless than he would have to ask. Lynn and that SOB Russell Aiken were right: she had Teletubby eyes.

Her hand tappity-tapped on Michael's police sketch.

"Lookit: Michael's out of reach," said Silas. "I know where he's headed because I know what Kolya wants from him. The endgame for Baku will be competing pipelines. It will be the Black Sea oil for us and the keys to Central Europe. I have a reasonably good idea the Russians will counter with a promise and a push for a second Nord Stream. Europe will bluster and barter and we *will* be prepared for that. But, overtly or covertly, China's kaleidoscope is operational. While everyone is preoccupied with their Spratley Islands cabbage patch aggression, they're going to move in Baku against us, or Kalaydoskop, or both at once.

"Now I must get going. I have a funeral to attend."

128 ACRES OF GARDENS and graves, of graceful statues, laughing fountains, and forbidding family crypts, dark-doored mausoleums and, if you like equations, at a standard yield of 1,000 graves per acre, well, there's doubtless some joker who will drive by today and wisecrack to his wife, his kids, in his best Bazooka Joe bubblegum comic strip wrapper impersonation—

"People who live around here can't be buried there."
"Why not? It's too crowded?"
"No. They have to be dead first."

Yuck, yuck, but in the case of the Fairfax, Virginia, Memorial Park, not far off the mark—their yearly intake averages four to five burial/funeral services each day.

Silas Kingston made one stop on his way to the cemetery. A shop he discovered online. A kind of artsy-fartsy gift store of useless hippy crap. He selected what he knew they sold, what he needed for the funeral, and arrived late at the Vale of Serenity.

Took a seat on a stone bench backed against a privacy barrier of pink-blossomed camellias. Two tall dogwoods, at the end of their second bloom, gently rained creamy white petals Silas could almost hear hitting the paved walkway as he sat alone facing a short row of seven graves. He waited.

Although there was no funeral, another mourner arrived. She double-taked to discover she was not alone. She gave Silas, the stranger, a curious, sad-owl look. Went to the grave she came to visit each week. The grave with the newest flowers. Replaced them with a fresh bouquet she pulled from her floral pattern tote bag. Silas scooted to the far-left end of the bench. Motioned, the rest of it was free.

She smiled at the stranger, distracted. Placed her tote between them. Next to Silas's brown-bagged gift. He pulled it a little closer.

A minute went by before she said, "I'm sorry to intrude, but have I seen you here before?"

He turned his most sympathetic face her way. Blinked moist eyes. He said, "Mary was your daughter?"

"Yes."

"I have a daughter. Only a few years different in age."

"Is she...?" Embarrassed, her finger brushed air at the headstones.

"Thankfully, no... But almost."

"I see."

They gazed wanly at one another. As strangers encountering each other in graveyards often do. You might call the woman "elderly", but she was younger than Silas. She reached into her tote, and while she hunted something, Silas adjusted. Not much of an adjustment at all; just a within-reach scooch. From a distance, they now would appear a couple.

She set to knitting. A sweater for a small child.

"That's lovely. You have a talent."

"Thank you. It's for her son. Poor child." She nodded at her daughter's grave. Pulled a pair of scissors. Cut her yarn.

"New?" Silas nodded at the scissors.

She hid it well, but Silas sensed tension radiate from her every pore. He focused on her daughter's grave.

"I used bufalin," he said. "It's a cardiotonic steroid toxin. Originally, it would have been isolated from Chinese toad venom, but we created this in a lab." His hand drifted into his gift bag. "I thought the Chinese component—you having been in their employment at Dulles—had a kind of symmetry, and—"

The scissors flashed for his throat. Silas was far too quick. Seized her wrist with his left hand.

Grit teeth: "I wanted you to suffer your daughter—"

—as his right appeared from the paper bag gripping a colorful, cylindrical, crystal rod meant to be pulled through the perpendicular, kaleidoscope tube he flung away with a violent shake.

"—As you would have had me suffer the death of mine."

The old woman was younger. She was strong. Enraged. Possessed of a bizarre fighting urge rather than flight instinct. He released her wrist. She thrust black scissors he parried with the crystal wand, purposely shattering it against the twin blades, giving it the jagged edge he drove into her soft throat, hard and deep and fatal.

He pushed her back across the bench. He used her little artsy-craftsy sweater to wipe his prints from the crystal shaft protruding from her throat. Stood over her until she belonged only there.

⚜⚜⚜

Silas slowed as he dropped below the Maryland 235/Prince Frederick Road, southbound on the 5. He hit his flashers. Cruised onto the shoulder. Rolled to a stop at the *Junction 32* highway sign.

Since August, a bit of yellow fabric had fluttered from a fresh splinter in the weathered old post. He'd checked it since, and it had always been where it was.

Today he removed it. Stuffed it into his shirt pocket. Got back into his Cadillac. Continued home to Foxtail Farm.

Clive

1.

FOR CLIVE LANCER, THIS summer afire had gone from the hotfoot of an unexpected crush to a leap over a beer-bong bonfire he should have been nowhere near; from the fireworks of first love—damn, it killed him that's what this was—to the personal/professional holocaust it had all become.

Paige caught me with her mother's hand literally *on my cock.*

Halfway over the garden wall, it was like that *where-did-it-all-go-wrong?* freeze frame movie moment. Left hand flat atop the parapet, arm bent, muscles gathered. Right arm extended, free. Light for balance. White dress shirt open. Blousing. Chest scorched where he'd invited Gwen in, heart beneath, molten from where Paige already lived.

And left?

Knees tucked. Paired parallel. Momentum ready to propel him into the impossibly lush-leafed, orange-fruited citrus trees of the withered, boarded-window mansion of Garde-Joyeuse.

The fucking Listening Post.

Right next door to the Silas Kingston Foxtail Farm.

"Men sometimes have to sacrifice to make hard deci-sions for a greater cause."

Her eyes convey more fire than the red sequins and glass beds of her startling dress.

"When you become a man—one without a pull-string—you'll understand exactly how true that statement is and how hardcore you failed it tonight."

A perfect vault; a freeze-frame on failure/fuck-up. Humiliation. Desolation. Her words augur for his doom. That perched moment, hand on the wall, body airborne, thoughts tumbling to the ground faster than he, and it struck him: the whole "pull-string" bit. The programmed responses of a child's action-figure doll. People pulling and Clive always ready-answered, hiding behind his perfect lie. Never meaning/believing/caring for a word of it; always the right response for whatever people needed. All his life.

And why not? It all came terribly easy. Had gotten him from an impoverished, one bedroom Road Town apartment on Tortola, British Virgin Islands, to univer-sity in London. To recruitment into the UK's Secret Intelligence Service—the bloody James Bond MI6—an honest-to-God, real-life, secret agent planted in the garden of an American considered CIA royalty. He'd cheated the rules chasing Paige and by that, had lifted a stone and discovered her geezer grandfather might very well/most likely/probably-fucking-*is* one of the great-est turncoat/traitor snakes in US/UK/former USSR espi-onage history.

Clive Lancer: bottom man on the ladder, already with a crowning achievement within his grasp...were he not entirely in over his head.

Had been his entire life.
Where did it all go wrong, mate?
You know where.
Day one. Born with this damned sodding brain.

WHAT'S THE OLD CHESTNUT—*Out of the frying pan, into the fire?* For Clive Lancer, that one had always been *out of the fire…into a blaze.* And the cliché—*He was far too clever for his own good?* Apply it to young Lancer as well. But not the way the cliché intends. Usually, the "far too clever" fellow gets tagged once he's gone *too* far. Gotten mercilessly burned. Clive preferred stealthy shortcuts over the patient application of intellect. Always. Delighted in them. Of course, if one's intellect only goes so far, a person is bound to get torched early enough in life to save themselves from an adult existential inferno.

Clive's problem?

He didn't possess that safety rail. That only-so-far fire insurance level of intelligence. Clive's mind operated on a whole other level of intelligence.

Biographical context: *Ms. Lancer, home early one evening from the third of the three jobs she holds to hold her small family together, observes son Clive playing the card game 500 with Grand-mère Amie.*

Grand-mère Amie: she's the elderly neighbor (not Clive's grandmother) who watches Clive and his half-sister Krystal. Not only is Clive playing this modified version of euchre, the fast-and-loose cousin of contract bridge, but he is speaking broadly and easily, sub-

versive bon-mots to Amie's glee, in the old woman's ancestral Gambian Wolof mixed with her St. Martin-native French.

Ms. Lancer is knocked for six. Clive rarely speaks his native English. Is abnormally silent. Is this some strange magic that goes on while she's ruining her hands scrubbing resort toilets? (Fundamentally—core soul/superstition level—she already knows it is.)

"Ah, Silvy-Silvia, the boy is fine. He's having a fun. I am a good teacher. If you or his sister would pay half the attention he do, I could teach you worlds of remarkable things."

Maybe. But Clive is only four years old. What she is witnessing is entirely unnatural. Queer and disquieting. And Sylvia Lancer fears it because what Sylvia Lancer doesn't say, is since the night Clive's father abandoned her and her daughter, she cursed herself. She has waited for this curse to manifest. That night, when the man she loved chose cards and gambling and a boat to who-knows-where (but nowhere good), Sylvia Lancer shorted her rent money, deposited Krystal with Grand-mère Amie, bought herself an expensive dinner, and went to the fancy tourist cineplex.

It was the night of the day she learned she was pregnant with Clive.

The film was Rain Man. *The character played by Dustin Hoffman attracted her, repulsed her—reminded her of her own father—and moved Sylvia deeply. Unlike any performance she ever witnessed. But when the plot moved to Las Vegas, and the story hinged upon gambling and cards as the only method available to save the two brothers, Sylvia knew the devil at work and fled the theater in fear.*

For four years, Sylvia has carried a premonition the movie somehow infected her and, through her living blood, infected her son sparked to life inside of her.

This night, inside of Grand-mère Amie's apartment—the cards and the seashell betting; the frightening, impossible speaking in tongues—this is her Rain Man *curse made manifest.*

The next morning, Sylvia Lancer takes her boy to have his head examined.

Forty-eight hours later (after stealing resort-tourist money to pay back that rent, thus sealing the curse): "Ms. Lancer, your child is not autistic. Far from it. And, I assure you, there is no such thing as a gambling gene. What you can *look forward to with young Clive is a remarkable child destined for great things—if reared properly. What you have been blessed with is a boy who will need constant mental stimulation and challenge. His IQ—and we've given him every preschool test available— It could not rank any higher."*

Ms. Lancer didn't know what that and a kettle of fish would get her boy, didn't trust this wasn't exactly another kind of curse, but she loved her son, and she respected a doctor's authority. She provided every opportunity available to support Clive's education. Allowed him to be tested each year, for the next five years, as he blazed through his primary grades. It was always the same amazement— *"This kid is a genius"*—and they steered him to genius-y things.

Clive would have preferred, *"This genius is a kid."*

Would have preferred his pursuits steered in more imaginative, playful, *outdoor* directions. He didn't appreciate being singled out. Segregated. Stuck solving problems that had no practical value to his life as he could already rationalize the world and his best place in it. How he observed it as a kid who lived on a beautiful island with the warm waters of a crystal sea lapping at white sand beaches where a vast variety of natural and physical pursuits—that *didn't* come easily—delighted and challenged him. Where his growth in strength and agility and coordination could increase at a natural and competitive rate with the age-appropriate companions of his youth.

Education, for Clive, was painful. Always changing schools, switching teachers, always moving up grades, always new doctors and abstract, unrewarding tests. No matter. Wherever they put him, Clive didn't fit. He didn't make friends with the older kids who avoided, ignored or teased him. Everything was weird to Clive, and he weirded-out everyone he was around. School was unnatural.

Age ten. A new battery of tests. Clive failed them on purpose. Not the first kid to pull that one. Called out on it. Asked, told, ordered to take it again until he played fair; the cajoling, the bribery, anger, and finally—after Clive went on total freeze-up/lockdown/locked-jaw strike—the surrender.

Powers-that-be weren't going to *be* anything anymore with Clive Lancer. Authorities allowed their investment in his schooling to come to a halt. Were it not for his mother's grief, Clive's next move: purposely fail out at the end of the term and, at ten, be done with school for good.

Were it not for Sylvia Lancer's grief, Clive would have failed his way into becoming a socially engineered underachiever. A BVI street/beach rat. But Clive loved his mother. Vowed to discover one thing about a scholastic education he could make his own and love as much as she loved him.

Clive discovered cheating.

What if you didn't do any work at all? Learned nothing on purpose but *still* performed better than anyone? The kids with the roving eyes, the blatant copying, the plagiarism—always caught. Shamed. Punished. Suspended. In its most basic applications, cheating was unsustainable as a methodology to carry oneself from scholastic achievement to academic success. Clive reasoned that was true, but only if a cheater—and all the cheaters he'd seen caught—was seeking an easy way out of an immediate problem by the onetime theft/false transfer of a single piece of denied information.

What if you flipped it? What if you approached cheating not as an easy way out, but the hardest way in?

A way into a protected system of information that exists inside of a secure complex of interlocking denied areas, protected documents, abstracts, and formulas, all timed to a specific order of secure events. All monitored by adults arrayed against you, trained in a specific set of behavioral surveillance methods and security measures.

It would involve deception. Would involve deceit. Theft of information through undetected surveillance. Charm came into play, as did seduction. (To be clear: "seduction" meant a little extra of the "Isn't he cute?"/

"Isn't he a flirt?"/ "Our Clive is a little devil," level of seducing *anyone*. Peer or professor).

As Clive grew better at cheating, the systems arrayed against him became more difficult to penetrate. Cover more precarious. Objectives more complex. The success he needed to meet his cheat-objective came to involve secret writing, smuggled documents, pilfered/copied/returned papers and answer keys.

Clive succeeded. Brilliantly. Near the top of his class in every class, he made it through five years of secondary school in four terms. Didn't think twice before enrolling into the elective pre-college study that kept him in school and out of the workplace—which without skills or non-criminal applicable knowledge was a mission unthinkable—he allowed his education to continue. The getting through was more of the same. It was the getting out—the oral exams—and the mission impossible of getting into a university where the first major obstacles of Clive Lancer's now seventeen years lay.

And it was too bad. Not only had Clive found a part of school he loved (as he had vowed to his mother), but that thing he loved—the great game of cheating—was fun. Granted, not as fun as spearfishing beneath the bay, boating or waterskiing on its surface, not as purely satisfying as swing bowling in beach cricket, kicking a football, or barefoot climbing the tallest palms for tourist dollars, but because he had no actual studies, no homework he ever did, Clive had more time than other young men his age for outdoor physical enjoyment. Soon, he had a body to match the natural good looks of his features. Women who always enjoyed his personality now wanted to enjoy his physique. And this, he quickly realized, was how he'd dazzle his way past his final oral exams.

♔ ♔ ♔

MADAME DIEUDONNE—the head of the Kingston Town, Baronville-Tower High School French Department—was a forty-two-year-old maiden who lived alone in the house of her deceased father, built by his father from the volcanic rock at the end of a high promontory cliff. Like all educators on Tortola, Mdm. Dieudonne had known of Clive Lancer from the beginning of his scholastic career; she'd watched him grow before her eyes—energetic youth to strapping young man—from the lofty paths of her lonely perch above the bay where Clive played and found his leisure; where Clive grew strong and came into his own in the blue-sky sunshine and diamond-dripping, sparkling sea.

Not unattractive herself, Mdm. Dieudonne had been, all her life, terribly too inquisitive around men. So anxious to like and be liked, she asked far too many questions, far too much of the time, and driven away every eligible man. When exactly Madame Dieudonne began to fantasize about Clive Lancer is unknown nor is it relevant (and, hopefully, more recently than not), but Clive would recall the first time he saw her in full sunshine on her lonely cliffside path. He, still a boy, would forever link that moment to the tingle on his toes dancing along the foam of a wave, and later, as boy-become-man, would remember it—not of her, but of the receding wave—as he peeled back the lace edge of her lingerie with tingling in his fingertips.

Spinster-single, Madame Dieudonne carried too much time in her empty, un-held hands. This had led her to an unwanted/unpaid/barely supervised executive position on the Caribbean Examination Council (CXC). The board which provides the regional and internationally recognized secondary school leaving examinations.

This was relevant to Clive.

He knew she watched him from her cliff, and she wasn't unappealing to a virgin boy.

What if I apply myself? This once. What if I pull some sort of Rain Man with Madame Dieudonne? Do something so extraordinary...

Mdm. Dieudonne would be Clive's first recruited asset. In their first meeting at her high school office, he admitted the truth: he had never studied French. Not a day of it, a minute, a bloody second. There was no record of it spoken in his family. His mother remembered the African dialect he'd spoken with Grand-mère Amie, but hadn't recognized the French all those years ago, and no one could ask the old St. Martin grandma because she'd since gone to her heavenly reward. Clive presented himself to Mdm. Dieudonne, his last year of pre-college coursework, and proclaimed he would take his scholastic "concentration" tests in French. He became her very own French prodigy and, for the sex-starved, sexually peaking maiden, her French tickler as well.

While Clive's mother had worried he was Dustin Hoffman in *Rain Man*, he emerged from a year of French studies under Mdm. Dieudonne (and ofttimes she under him) Bill Murray at the keyboard in *Ground-*

hog Day. His astonishing achievements in French made all the island papers and were picked up by the *Daily Mail* in the UK and worldwide.

Clive had never bothered with newspapers before, but after devouring the British tabloid, and the love stricken Mdm. Dieudonne, he decided his future would not be on the island of Tortola.

While he failed (legitimately) every other exam, the Madame made certain his test records, illegitimately, reflected the opposite. Clive was accepted into the University of Central Lancashire.

To cheat at a collegiate level was to slay a whole different dragon. Cleverness and charisma only got him halfway into its lair. University-level cheating required mad skills in forgery. In breaking and entering, the picking of classroom locks, labs, professors' desks. It involved computer hacking and data breach. Of scrambling rain gutters, scampering rooftops, lowering through windows to photograph the answers. It involved willing and unwilling student co-conspirators, and it required the manipulation, seduction and/or coercion of deans, tutors, teachers, and faculty. The bribery of custodial and physical plant labor. Collegiate espionage required a kind of devil-may-care charm that made everyone around you whom you were cheating and/or compromising impulsively and involuntarily want to see you succeed.

As an intellectual pursuit, the challenges Clive met and mastered at university were off-the-charts fun. England was fun. Europe, assumably more fun. And the rest of the world—which included several Disneylands—an entire Disneyland for Clive's audacious and oddly/entirely naïve joie de vivre.

Why *wouldn't* he cheat his way into the Foreign Service?

2.

"Who's this git believe he's fooling?"

"I'd say everyone. Everywhere. Whole life."

"Which he has obviously cheated his way through. This is unacceptable. He is unacceptable."

"The fact we're discussing Mr. Clive Lancer on a stack of records and recommendations better achieved, assembled, put forth than most legitimate applicants— The fact he's made it through every gate and gatekeeper but this last vetting of ours, leads me to believe—"

"He lied to us! To our recruiters. His interviewers. Shamelessly."

"Shamelessness is not unknown to our profession. Matter o'fact we instill—"

"He lied on his polygraphs."

"He beat his polygraphs."

"They weren't the ones you're supposed to beat!"

"Yet, he got away with it to make it this far. To us—"

"Us! That's right—us. The last gatekeepers. Final defense. We two, bound in duty to put an end to Clive Lancer."

"Hmm. Not feeling it." Chin rub here. Reflective tilt of the head. "For our work, I'd say Clive Lancer might be

*the most acceptable candidate we've had since you and
I have been doing this."*

"Not sure I care to follow."

*"He's already done—with admirable success his en-
tire life—what we take years to train our recruits to do
half-as-well as we have him starting out. Cost: nuthin'."*

*"Well, that's just fine. That's just marvelous. I'll tell
you this: he won't be able to cheat his way through Fort
Monckton. Clive Lancer will wobble out broken the first
week of drill."*

Six months later, Clive completed his infantry training
and his unconventional warfare course at the top of his
form.

He dreamt of Paris. Of berets and cafes and trench
coats. Clive dreamed sultry girls who smoked Gitanes.
He got Hollywood Township, Maryland, and Fergus
Jones.

♛ ♛ ♛

LIKE A CAT or a cat burglar or a thief of hearts, Clive
landed un-wobbly on the other side of the Kingston
wall. A sprint across the dark and untended property,
out the gate to his car, back to his Super 8 motel room
on Route 235. He waited for Fergus to storm the stairs
and burst through the door. To threaten and throttle. To
haul him away in irons. To chop off his head and fuck
his throat with a butcher knife.

He waited. Didn't move—except for water and to
piss—two days. Scared shitless.

Night of July thirteenth. Fergus tap-tapped the air-conditioner-fogged window as he walked past to the door where he politely knocked.

"Decent in there, Clive-y, my boy? Pair of us need ourselves a little chit-chat."

What was it Paige said when I talked about quitting? "Do they even let you? They must reel you back in and don't let you walk moonlight beaches with American girls whose grandpa you've been trying to trap."

♛♛♛

BACK ON THE NIGHT OF JULY ELEVENTH, less than five minutes after Clive raced off in his dinky rental with his limp dick dinky, Fergus fired off a terse, though no less seething, report to his Operations Supervisor.

Young Lancer had made a cock-up of their mission. Failed to screw his way into the wet/warm comfort of the Kingston lap. Compounded the disaster by breaking operational security and fleeing directly into the LP (not exactly true). Furthermore, strong evidence Fergus included suggested the cowardly fool may have compromised his cover to the Kingston granddaughter. (True, but he didn't *know* it.)

Action needed to be taken. Something conclusive. Stakes too high, and Fergus come too far. A dozen years he'd put into Silas Kingston. He didn't need to remind anyone. Made a point of doing so with capital letters and underlines. Fergus requested, as a demand, the authority to terminate Clive Lancer's employment with the service and anywhere else in the future that would require a living, breathing body.

Upon receipt and review, his Operation Supervisor abdicated the dirty missive to his Division Manager. He armored himself with an "anonymous" from extralegal affairs.

A secure, four-way call followed something like this:

OPS SUPER: "So much untapped potential, that young man."

DIV MGR: "Everything came easily to him."

FERGUS: "I warned you: he never took our work here seriously."

OPS SUPER: "No. It appears he didn't push himself."

FERGUS: "And when push came to shove—the wanker popped."

OPS SUPER: "He fizzled."

DIV MGR: "He zeroed. No drive. Never had it."

"ANONYMOUS": "He was already breaking thin ice."

FERGUS: "Why you dropped him on my head—don't deny it. 'Crazy old Fergus chasing Cold War ghosts.' This was the Wally's last chance."

"ANONYMOUS": "The annoying part, Fergus, is you told him. You gave him the 'why' about Kingston. You'd been advised not to."

FERGUS: "I didn't take the advice. He needed a push."

"ANONYMOUS": "It hasn't landed any of us into a place we want to be."

FERGUS: "Whatever we do, we can't have him wandering around with his hands in his pocket while he whistles a tune that if anyone asks, he knows all the lyrics."

DIV MGR: "Yes. That is the murky water we find ourselves treading."

"ANONYMOUS": "Murky water's where the sharks always wait."

FERGUS: "If it's Extreme Measures looking back at us from the water's reflection, waters 'round here are deep. Nothing dropped in would wash up at Brighton." A breath's space. Added, "I don't need anyone else, 'specially fool Lancer, to finish getting the rest of what I need on Silas Kingston before the real doing gets done."

"ANONYMOUS": "There's no one more extremely suited to all aspects of this affair after all these years than you. We do value that."

OPS SUPER: "It's always been a question of brotherhood."

DIV MGR: "Brotherhood with the service. Admirable."

FERGUS: "The service be damned. To my own flesh and blood. That's what's kept me at this, year in and year out, when none but the Queen believed in me. In this work—this American's heinous crimes. Justice for my brother is the only question I'm concerned with. The 'answer' I will finally deliver to Silas Kingston on order of Her Majesty—which we all know she will grant."

"ANONYMOUS": "Do we? Not sure that's under royal purview. These last, uh, hundred or so years, Mr. Fergus Jones."

Fergus chuckled, and we say hyenas laugh, and there is nothing to find funny in either.

FERGUS: "She weren't at your baptism though. Standing in for your brother. Promising your Deddy."

Had they been in person rather than on secure teleconference from Vauxhall Cross, they would, like recognizing Fergus's laugh, have wanted to call his expression a smile, but knew that smile, his smile, was a thing that scared them.

OPS SUPER: "Yes. Right. There is that."

And that bothered everyone. After consultation with the Chief, with consultation of the Foreign Secretary, it all swung back to the Operation Supervisor who transmitted orders to Fergus Jones plowing rocks of bitterness and vengeance in his jealously guarded plot of the field.

👑 👑 👑

CLIVE THOUGHT NOTHING GOOD would come from answering the door. Fergus rapped again. Leaned out. Looked in. Grinned at Clive through the window. Waved, bouncing his fingers all together like you do. *Hi, wittle baby.* A hand clapping itself at an infant. Reluctantly, Clive opened the door.

Their eyes measured each other across the threshold. Failure in Clive's, the malice of happy-hell in Fergus's. Clive hung his head.

Fergus patted his cheek. "Cheer up, boy. You earned yourself a ticket home."

"Tortola?" He could hear the seagulls' cry.

His request for a solution to Clive Lancer that he could live with (by which Clive would not), denied, Fergus grit yellow teeth and hum/hissed through them, "Little closer to Big Ben." Cleared his throat. "Be quick about it. Get your things. You'll need to do a wee bit of damage control for the other night. Lay some cover on your jilted Jilly's boon companion, then off we go."

ARRIVED LONDON, 11:30ish, July 15. Fergus and Clive to baggage claim. Bustle busy with big bag vacation travelers, with the pump shotgun *clack-clack* of international business folks' hand-rollers cocked before tromping importantly (to themselves and only themselves) for the train, to cars, to their bored and waiting spouses, to the diffident drivers with name placards jockeying for position with the unctuous tour guides brandishing the flag-stick signs like lancers.

This Lancer, Clive, grabbed his duffel. Fergus pointed to his bag and Clive grabbed it too as the Minjerowns—as in *"Min'jer'own bloody business who they are, you twat. You're deep enough in the shite as is!"*—three expressionless men, suits and sunglasses, appeared as escorts, circled as hounds. Hustled them to an SUV—the menacing black beasts favored equally by the SIS and the Londongrad oligarch crowd.

"Get in," said Fergus. Clive got in.

"Get out." 2 p.m. the Hotel Corbin. A loud, shitty—as in the odor of fresh dog crap that never dissipated for as long as Clive boarded, or, better, was boarded-in; loud—as in the yapping dog, the foul-mouthed owner and his wife, herself an adept at mimicking the full variety of traffic brakes that never came to a stop until they collided with her husband's temper—Peckham, London, hotel. If there were other guests or other prisoners like himself, Clive had no knowledge. The Minjerowns—who had searched his duffel on the hearse-quiet ride into the city—tossed it on the bed, prodded him in after it, and locked Clive inside his room upon arrival.

Following morning, 7 a.m. exactly, the door unlocked. Two of his Minjerowns waited in the shabby, poop-fragrant hallway. No one spoke. One of the pair jerked his head. Clive left the door ajar. Went back inside his room. He splashed his face. Threw on a suit, but not a tie—leash for one of these menacing mutts to tug on—and allowed himself to be handled into the SUV. Driven away.

Swooped to the MI6/SIS Building. South bank of the River Thames, Vauxhall. Postmodern and sarcastically known as Legoland. Been there once before for a hollow welcome aboard and a "Here… Here…and here. And here," final papers signing.

Pleasant office.

Nice to see those papers again, too.

Pristine pages, edges neat and tight and—

Probably should have read them—

—never touched or referred to once.

Like nuclear weapons.

There was a jolly, red-cheeked fellow with a mustache bristly on his upper lip in a way that made it appear it had been full until this morning when he trimmed it but forgot to shave the stubble. Maybe a moment of *Look at the time— Spend any more on this, I'll be late to terrorizing Clive Lancer with my chuckling Bob's Your Uncle routine.*

"One Sally in one hand, one in the other, birthday cake on your breath, three-way fun—if candle wishes come true and American internet movies prove real—"

makes the sign of the cross, beady eyes at his ceiling—
"Yet off our Calypso Connery goes, yelping and clutching his britches."

"They're mother and daughter."

"They're American."

Clive clenched his jaw and boiled. Jolly Jack (wasn't his name—the Jack part—or maybe it was; he never introduced himself), grinned and wiggled eyebrows. Brushy like his lip crawler.

"You'd like to sock me? Punch ol' Ruddy Cheeks in the nose? Get on the next boat to your coconut tree lagoon?" Sudden seriousness, the moustache suddenly sinister. "You know that's never going to happen. Ever."

"You can ask me to resign. Fire me."

"We would, but Fergus told you something he shouldn't."

"Don't those papers cover that? My obligation to forgetting?"

The man twiddled his thumbs.

"C'mon," Clive smirked. "Everyone leaves with secrets."

"Not people like you. Not with secrets like this."

Twiddling continued.

Clive pointed at the man's caterpillar thumbs. "That's extra obnoxious of you. Thanks." But it was getting to him. "Are you planning on putting me in prison?"

"It would be better than the Fergus Jones alternative."

His thumbs struck together, tip to tip, as though creating an electric circuit that shocked Clive and widened his eyes.

"Obviously, *we*—" he swirled a hand in the air as though conjuring everyone of importance in the building into his answer—"don't allow that, don't participate in *that*...but..."

"That's why you call it the 'Fergus Jones Alternative'?"

"Lots of names for lots of things. I can't keep them straight."

Clive managed his broadest smile. "You're fuckin' with me."

Jolly Jack/ol' sinister Ruddy Cheeks made his third transformation. Normal. Real. Serious. "Clive, take this any way you like, but I am the person assigned to you—not by choice/no choice—*assigned* to make this as right as it can be made *for* you. I'm the other guy now, on your losing team. Problem for me is, I look at everything we know about you—and we know *everything*—and honestly, I don't know why someone didn't expect something like this with you in the first place and bar the door. But maybe they did, and it's why they put you on an operation that was not going to go anywhere and was never going to go anywhere—*never* supposed to—until you came along and flipped the bloody script."

His face drooped, chin dropped, head like a balloon lost of air. Beady eyes waited.

"I had nothing to do with Silas Kingston and his radio call to Moscow—or wherever."

"Ah. But if you hadn't been chasing his granddaughter, you'd have already been gone from the listening post and none of this..." He spread his hands.

Kind of a Jesus-y gesture. That's the thing that broke Clive. He sank in abjection into his chair. The man rose, body round as his face, and came around behind Clive. Squeezed his shoulders a couple times. And, since he didn't fire a gun into the back of young Lancer's head, made Clive a wee bit better. After the terror he was going to fire a gun, subsided.

"The way I see this, Clive," he circled back to his chair. "You're my Pinocchio and I've been put on you to be your Jim-cracky Cricket."

"That doesn't fill me with confidence."

"Me neither. But right now, you're still made of wood and Fergus is stoking the basement boiler fires. The only thing you have on him or any of *us*—" again with the circular *means all of us* hand motion— "is before you went off with Gwen Kingston, you spent at least two hours without eyes-on in the company of Silas Kingston. A cake and ice cream jolly."

"So what?"

"So, without lying to me, tell me everything he said, everything he did, everything you—"

"He didn't say or do anything."

"You don't know it; he doesn't know it; and I don't know it...yet. But he did. And I am going to untangle your strings before someone wraps them around your throat."

"I didn't notice him until we all sat at the outside picnic table, and he came out of the separate house where he lives carrying a bottle and joined—"

"A bottle of what?"

"Who knows?"

"Did you drink any?"

"Yes!"

"Well, what was it?"

"I dunno, brandy. No, cognac."

Jolly Jack/Ruddy Cheeks/Jim-Cracky Cricket shoved a legal pad toward Clive. Offered a pencil. "Draw the table. Where everyone sat. Then we'll go into what you were talking about before he arrived—who said what and to whom—and how the conversation moved once Silas took his seat."

Clive rolled his eyes to hide the panic in them. "I don't see this helping me. What's stopping me from making shit up?"

"You know the phrase, 'You can't cheat the hangman?' I'm the hangman...unless you help me off the gallows."

♔ ♔ ♔

JOLLY JACK— Strike it. Ruddy cheeks— Cross it out. Same with the Disney-fied Carlo Collodi Talking Cricket. An "anonymous" from extralegal affairs, Anton Hector acted as one of three hangmen on cases where cause for a fatal solution presented itself as the best option for a troubled/troublesome officer. It was not a solution often considered, let alone taken; there were not, as books and movies and television suggest—strike *that*—rely upon, roving in-house hitmen standing ready behind every topiary for any field officer who makes a false step. Prison is what was real. Even for the worst traitors. But there were some instances where something quicker and cleaner and permanent was necessary. Was misty eyes-on-the-Union-Jack vital. These cases were examined independently by a three-person, lowercase A, "anonymous" panel searching for a path to *leniency*. Unknown to each other, each made a report and cast a vote that would render a majority solution none of them would ever know.

One of the "anonymous" had been on the SOS call from Fergus; this individual was looking at the operation in toto going all the way back to Moscow, 1971. There was Anton, Clive's hangman, and there was a third "anonymous" simultaneously putting Fergus under the microscope. They would take all summer if they had to, and with this, they did.

In his sixteen years with the SIS, Anton had worked on eight of these cases. On three, he'd voted for extreme measures. The other five, leniency. He had no idea how any of them played out.

This case of Clive Lancer, his ninth, was the weakest of them all.

The deeper he dug into Clive's story, the saddest and most unfair. They wouldn't even be considering this were it not for the one factor that made all his efforts to save Clive moot. Her Royal Highness the Queen of England, Elizabeth II, by the Grace of God, of the United Kingdom of Great Britain and Northern Ireland and of her other realms and territories Queen, Head of the Commonwealth, Defender of the Faith, had—since a mechanic doffed and clutched his cap to meet her as a princess—befriended her as her first sergeant. He shaped her into an officer, taught her engine repair at Camberley in 1945, and became the kind face of her World War. Her Majesty took a personal stake in vengeance against Silas Kingston.

Against a queen, an island cheat like Clive Lancer didn't stand a chance.

Monday, October Twenty-ninth

1.

Bone weary. Blood ache. Molecular exhaustion. In fever dream delirium, Michael wandered surreal landscapes horrific. Insects from the smallest parasitic worm to scuttling, hard-jawed/soft-bellied creatures the size of monsters, and in all the forms of man, in the millions, billions, if not trillions—turbulent and tumultuous—beset and bedeviled him but could not engulf Michael. Could not overwhelm him because they could not move.

Each was a locus of fire. The world an inferno. Every bush burned. Every city, a pillar of fire. The air, choked with flaming flies, mosquitoes, moths, and wasp, blazed in sheets and waves and whorls. In Michael's dream, insect fire was the air itself. His lungs consumed it. Fire fed his blood, and his blood fed his life, and fire was the thing that cleansed and purified him.

Ten days after he collapsed on the doctor's doorstep, Michael said goodbye to Helene Favre, and answered his mother's voice.

"Michael... Michael... Honey, wake up."

"Here, Mom. I'm awake."

His eyes opened. He gazed, reborn, upon her face alive. Her pale skin made the speckled flush of her cheeks stand out vivid and red. Her eyes—a darker blue than he remembered, highlighted with diamond cerulean crypts—grew moist. Glimmered delight. The peace of love.

Kaleidoscope-patterned. Unblinking. Vivid. Confident.

Her lips spread, fixed in a smile. Overwhelmed now overcome. Hopeful with joy. Alive and real.

"Mom?"

When did I last see you smile? Hardly once during your cancer. In my heart, I declared you dead while you lay, still breathing, in your bed.

Like Michael, Doris lay in a medical bed. In her arms: an infant.

A photograph. Of course it is. Stupid. So tired. Crushed and sick.

Michael sensed another presence in the room. He remembered to speak in Russian. "How long have I been here?" His voice was sandpaper.

A delicate hand. Plastic cup. Metal straw with a flexible rubber end. Michael drank.

"Ten days. Your fever broke last night."

Michael lay in a hand-crank portable medical bed. An IV stand ran two intravenous lines.

"Infusion fluids. Antibiotics." The back of his hand. Crook of his elbow.

"Why am I here?"

"You chose a most difficult way to make the trip."

"Don't fuck with me." Michael gestured with the photograph in the slide-in/Plexi-frame propped in his free hand; arm bent across his stomach. "Is that me?"

"The baby?"

"What is with you? I know who my mother is."

The doctor pinched his lips into a smile. Like he was biting a cranberry half-in, half-out of his mouth.

"You took this picture—I'm guessing you delivered me. Did you take pictures of every baby you delivered?"

"Important ones."

"Heh," Michael grunted. "I was an important baby. That's something." He stared at the picture of his mother, many years dead.

No color in the photo. No pink in her cheeks. No blue her eyes. No red lips—what'd Dad used to say—? The kind you see once in your life and live to kiss forever?

Frozen. Black-and-white. Like life and death—or maybe the other way around.

A dream. A ghost.

When he wasn't smiling, the doctor's lips remained pinched-cranberry-small while the rest of his face appeared large and ripe; it recalled to Michael the Arcimboldo portraits—dreadful heads composed entirely of fruits and vegetables—in the doctor's case spilling over the basket of his jaw in jowls and dewlaps. Michael wanted to dislike, even hate the man, but the warty pumpkin gourd of his head, the wrinkled walnut-shell eyes, his tomatoey cheeks and odd little cranberry mouth, the remarkableness of his goblin visage held Michael's vision long enough for him to see, better appreciate, what his patients had known him for: a gentleness that glowed from an inner light like a

Jack-o'-lantern. He was fascinating to look at, and the combination of rough exterior and warm lit core combined to an overwhelming sense of honesty.

He introduced himself as Dr. Dosifey Kiselyov, giving Michael's hand a squeeze with his delicate hand, pale and cold and moist as if recently washed, which his hands always were, although the rest of him, his clothing, his furnishings, the air in his rooms, smelled of decades of sharp cigarettes and sweet boiled tea, of faint sweat of a man who little bothered with bathing. He wore a cardigan, threadbare corduroys and house shoes. His legs crossed at the knee, seated in an armchair matched to some other room.

"I want to know the truth about my mother. About her and the Russian codenamed Kalaydoskop."

"Does the name Nikoláj Yurenev mean anything to you?"

"Just like that? That's him?"

"Kolya, to his friends."

"I'm not."

"I wasn't either."

"I'll never be. He's haunted my family as long as I can remember. Though I'm the only one who doesn't pretend he's not real."

A pointed look. "Your mother called him Kolya."

The fear of mortality—his own, his mother's gone—the pretending against it which composes every second of a conscious life, twisted in the pit of Michael's stomach. He expressed it with a smirk. He said, "And I've been lured here for you to tell me that affectionate name and whatever else they shared has everything to do with this?" He jigged the photo like a tambourine. Slapped the frame beside the filtered water pitcher on the small table beside him. "Talk."

"At this point in our conversation—before a compact is entered—let it suffice, at the time of your birth, I was a member of the Communist Party of the Soviet Union. For economic/lifestyle reasons. I am not a political man and abhor politics in all forms. I was never part of the state security apparatus. But, for creature comfort reasons, I worked for the KGB delivering the children of high-level intelligence officers."

"You're ridiculous. You wouldn't have delivered me. My parents would never have crossed paths with you."

"Not voluntarily. I'd never seen your mother before. After I took the photograph, I never saw her again. My involvement in your life and your mother's is miniscule, but if I tell you—my small part in it—it will change how you see yourself."

"You've already suggested the biggest change possible between the people we're discussing. Not that I believe it."

"*That* I don't know. I've not been told it. But Yurenev was with your mother when she went into labor. Your father was not."

Michael rolled his eyes. He pressed the back of his head into his pillow. Stared at the water-stained ceiling.

"But we get ahead of ourselves. I am to tell you what you hear from me will lead you deeper into a place you may not return from. Your life as you know it. As you cherish it. You understand me?"

Michael, his scowl drawing all the way from his eyes, from his furrowed brow beneath his shaggy hair. Boyish, he shrugged.

"Any peace you may have had over your closest relationships—may have not appreciated as you should have—you may never find it again."

Bone weary. Blood ache. Molecular exhaustion.

The Enchanted Forest.

A man kisses his mother, a man not his father.

Michael fought tears. Took in the room where his life—

Doris, Helene, Gwen, Lynn—God as Father Cevik—

My daughters I have abandoned to my pride

—had brought him. A spare bedroom. A modest and depressingly nondescript mid-century building. A guest bed in a cherry-stained particle board frame pushed against the wall. Spare furniture, nothing matching. Window curtains, old, sun-faded, in need of replacing years ago. Long without a woman's touch. Storage boxes.

"I won't betray my country. If that's what you people have in mind."

"That specific question is not what I'm led to believe our conversation will be about for you."

"What is it about?"

"Yurenev wishes you no ill will. He asked me to ask you if you remember the balloon he gave you."

Michael bounces the red balloon in the air. Turns. The sun bounces off its bright surface.

Sees his father. Weak, pathetic, and impotent.

The stranger, Yurenev—Kolya—kissing his mother. Doris kissing him back.

"Nope."

"He also instructed me to offer you these." From inside his sweater, he withdrew an Aeroflot ticket. "There is a diplomatic pass that goes with this. It will get you to the United States. You would be on your own with American Customs."

Michael laughed.

"What is funny?"

"This is the best inducement to recruitment I've ever seen played."

Dr. Kiselyov gave a ponderous headshake. "I told you. I'm not recruiting you to anything. The business you both are in is obscene."

"Maybe. But his offer hints what you have to trade is worth more than my escape to freedom."

"Would you like my advice as your doctor? No good will come from what I will tell you. While true to what I witnessed, it is purely circumstantial."

"Circumstances of my birth."

A single nod from the doctor.

"If it turns out you've lied to me, I will kill you."

"You would have every right to take my life. I was prepared to take both yours and your mother's."

Michael waited for time to stop; for heaven to let him off the hook. Time. Kept. Ticking.

"...Go on."

"You mother was thirty-five weeks pregnant. She was alone."

"My father's embassy work involved travel. He was a Publications Procurement Officer. His job was to buy books and encyclopedias, textbooks, magazines—anything from bookstores, newsstands—Moscow and other cities."

"Yes. I'm sure. The point is, he traveled and was five days going on six outside the city. I'm told your mother received permission to go shopping. At one of the Beryozka stores. From there, a rendezvous. It had all been planned."

"Yurenev. Kalaydoskop."

"Yes. He was unlike any other KGB. Those, no matter rank, whom I observed him encounter... He was not normal. They deferred, or, if they could, retreated. I witnessed this; the security services avoided his presence whenever they could."

"Who was he to Doris, my mother?"

"He was a book critic. A 'cover' in your line of work, I suppose. As a writer, he was celebrated. Because of that celebrity, he had much foreign access. How, he says, he met your father and your mother."

"We would have known. My father would have known. Would have known what else he did. A meeting like you describe—she would have been under our own observation. It would never have taken place. Ever."

The doctor spread his hands. "I wasn't there. I was only told that was the plan, and I waited in the kitchen where they slipped away for tea."

"She would never have done such a thing."

"I believe you. But I also know it happened. I drugged her food with enough synthetic oxytocin that she went into labor while she ate cake. Her water broke on their way outside where I was waiting in the ambulance. We took her to the Moscow Central Clinical Hospital, where I practiced."

"That's not what my birth certificate says."

"Your American birth certificate. With your birthday of September third." He met and held Michael's gaze.

"You were born on the second. While your father was in Tula."

"Recruiting a spy."

"I am aware. So was Yurenev and the recruitment went the other way. Once we set up at hospital, I administered tocolytics to slow your birth. Your father was located by telephone, and I prepared for two eventualities. He would agree with what Yurenev proposed and you would be born. Or he would not agree, and you and your mother would die."

"What did he agree to?"

Dr. Kiselyov gave a pointed look at the storage boxes.

"Everything you want to know about your father is inside those boxes. They're officially sealed. I have not opened them, and I do not want to see what they contain."

Michael rose halfway from the bed. "So, on the threat of my life, and my mother's, Kolya Yurenev, made my father into a traitor. A double agent."

"You don't seem surprised."

"I remember the balloon."

Michael crashed back into his pillows. Once again, stared at the ceiling. Projected, invisible, his childhood, his life, his memories of Doris onto the once white, yellow-stained surface.

Whatever's in those fucking boxes, Dad... None of my business. If it's true: I get it.

He didn't think about his mother. Her ghost, dead; the living ghost he knew as Kalaydoskop. The balloon man.

"This isn't anything that changes my life." Michael lied. Shook his head. Struggled to convince himself. A hard look at Kiselyov. "Not the way you people want it."

His eyes dared the old man to continue.

When Kiselyov spoke, it was barely audible. "We can be finished." He feigned interest in the pills on his sweater. "These last days. I received what a religious man would call a blessing." He looked deeply into Michael's face. "I saved your life. From a death as certain as the cowardly one I would have given you and your mother."

"You're not blessed. You're a son of a bitch and you always will be."

The goblin-headed doctor came to his feet. Scratched his back. "I've made us some soup."

An ordinary fellow would have cut it off there. But Michael was a Kingston. Reared in all things to be above the common. There will always be in people such born, an impulse much stronger than grace, more powerful than forgiveness, to take the extraordinary about themselves and hack at it until it reveals the tragedy at its center.

"It's the other thing." Michael's hurt voice held the doctor at the door. "The thing you said you witnessed. Say it."

The pinched cranberry lips. "No good, no good, no good..."

"Say it."

"I can only tell you what I witnessed. I have no other context. No medical evidence."

"Fucking what? Say it!"

He exhaled. Confessional. Dr. Kiselyov's posture opened. Voice flat, clinical. "You were a perfect baby. I cleaned you. I wrapped you. When I passed you to your mother, Yurenev said, 'My love. He's beautiful.' And your mother said, 'He has your eyes.'"

"I have children." Michael muttered, not believing what he said had meaning. "You can't tell what color their eyes are going to be."

"Your eyes. As an adult. Color, even the shape— They are remarkably similar to his."

Doris presses his cheeks between her hands. "Mine are blue. Dad's are brown. When you mix them, you get gray."

"Similar to how I remember them. He kissed her. She smiled. He said, 'Rest.' And he moved to leave."

"If I was his child, he would have killed her? The woman you say he loved. Us?"

"I had his order. I prepared the syringe for her. A scalpel for you." He whispered, incredulous to himself: "I would have done it without hesitation. Whatever else he is, he is that man as well."

The carousel. The red balloon. Lynn in her stroller.

Kolya Yurenev, kissing Doris, clocks Silas. Kisses Doris more deeply as his eyes meet Michael's.

We share the same eyes.

Michael lifts the frame. Stares. Searches his emotions.

"You want me to believe my mother was having an affair with a KGB officer— operation Kalaydoskop/Kaleidoscope—or whatever. Right. Got pregnant by him. Sure. Maybe even loved him. Okay, and here I am."

"I would say why you are here is because what you say, exactly, is what Yurenev wants you to believe. You don't have to. Even if it's biologically so. You never need know."

Michael stared at the photo a moment more. Put it aside. Bone weary. Blood ache. Molecular exhaustion.

"Was that everything?"

On the road, time had become elastic for Michael, but now, this was the moment it hardened into the permanence of everything before and all that would be after.

"No," the doctor said. "She told him, 'You know I won't—' No. I'm sorry. It was 'I can't.' Your mother said, 'You know I can't ever stop loving you.' And Yurenev said, 'This boy. Our boy. He proves that.'"

2.

*P*OP. *PLOP.* UHN! *POP-PLOP.* Uhn! *Pop-pop. Plop. Pop.* Uhn! *Pop*— If she didn't get aced on the serve, Lynn could hold her own on the clay. *Plop, plop, plop.* Game. Set—and three weeks into haunting the Rock Creek Tennis Club—match.

She carried an old membership, maybe fifteen years—how time flies—kept it on life support at the reduced rate for the gym-only which she never used because...alcohol. Upped it to full facility tennis/racquet sports and began arriving early each morning. Put her name on the pro shop white board. Picked up games/hitting partners. Lynn made a good singles "partner"—especially for the other women. No chit-chat, no come-on. Always competitive, adjusting and improving throughout the game; she'd win games but rarely sets and ultimately gave both her random partner and herself a vigorous workout. Lynn came back evenings—more the same—and weekends entirely.

By the second week, Lynn saw Aydin Sayadov enough times that friendly recognition progressed to "Hello" and "Hi" and even—from him— "Getting better and better. Enjoy your weekend," and Lynn smiled back from the sides of her smoothie straw.

Today, extra-early. First name on the board. A popular pick-up these days, Lynn made herself ready to go—racquet out/new ball-can out—grabbed a stool at a juice bar high-top. Buried her nose in her phone, texting herself (club rules: no voice calls allowed inside), and—"Work thing, sorry"—excused her way out of games until Aydin strolled inside from the valet. Looked like...tennis porn.

Lynn stowed her device. Bored-girl now. Looking around. Fiddled with her grip. Straightened her skirt. Fiddled, tweaking strings, looking around, whole time: eagle-eyed Aydin.

Out to the patio; craning his neck—all the courts, all the games, all the readies-and-waiting. Didn't find who he was looking for. Back inside. Checked with the desk. The headshake. Showed his phone, question mark face.

Nope. Gotta-gotta-go outside. Even gorgeous you...

He's out. A sympathetic but annoyed conversation.

What happens when your partner backs his car over a three-inch woodscrew I angled into his tread. Not a sidewall job. I'm kind. Ten bucks for a patch and good as new, but not gonna make your game...

Back inside.

Whatta-whatta-what to do? Yep. Aydin-Adonis: look at the board.

His long finger. Tap-tap. *Layla Kingsbury.* Swept his purple/gold Prada sunglasses. Landed on Lynn. She gave a wave. He mimed a racquet swing. *Give it a go?* A *Why not?* smile, and off the stool, onto the courts, racquet spin—

"Love serving love."

Pop! Unh! *Plop-pop!*

—and two entirely different games commenced play.

Juice bar. He went for lime spinach wheatgrass. Lynn/Layla: strawberry raspberry acai all the way. As Lynn promised herself, her legs led. Game-time—he'd noticed. More than once she swung them out from the juice bar stool. Crossed. Right leg lengthened over her left. A bounce now and then, and—

"They called it Key-lime pie with zest. Tastes a bit like they used the soap."

"They make Key-lime soap?"

"They make Zest, and they put it in this."

"I prefer my strawberry-raspberry without acai, but the withering judgment if I say, 'No acai.' I'm too wrung out from the court to withstand a volley from the juice barista—or whatever we're supposed to call them."

And a brush of her ankle against his calf.

"Well..." Aydin peered over his sunglasses. "You're supposed to call *me* 'gay.'"

Leg withdrawn. Cringe face. "Shit. Embarrassing."

"The you hitting on me, or the me being gay part?"

"If I say, 'You being gay,' does that give me another chance to try?"

Next to his looks, his laughter was a thing—real, healthy, strong—of beauty.

"Does it bother you I tried? I can't be the first."

"No. I like the trying—who wouldn't? If you were a man, the trying would lead to doing." He lifted his glass. She clinked it.

Lynn gave him a defiant look. "I'd be great as a gay man."

"The best there ever was, second only to your skill at typing."

This guy giving me Silas's bullshit?

Off her look: "*Stereo*-typing. Bitch."

Shit. He's pissed.

Aydin laughed again.

He's as good an actor as I am. Gear-shift: go.

"Aydin, I'm going to do normal for a second. You're in the car business. So I've heard."

Serious face. "How?"

"You've sold half the luxury cars in this lot."

"So, you didn't want in my pants, you want a deal on a car?"

"No. I did want in your pants—not gonna happen/got it—*and* I want a deal on a car. Or not. Or we can drop it. I can tell you about owning an H&R Block tax franchise. Or we can look at my Porsche—and scope out the valets and find out which of us's got better taste."

"I've tasted half of them."

Strawberry-raspberry acai went through Lynn's nose and his laughter rang like a bell.

"Who the fuck gets tipsy on Acai?" she said.

He offered his arm and escorted her to the parking lot.

♔♔♔

"Last year's Spyder. Low miles. Arctic Silver. You sure you want to sell this?"

"I know. It's flawless. Like me." Lynn did a game show hostess flourish. Got back a half-grin. "But I'd look better in a Mercedes."

"An SLS? Slick and fast. How you like it, yeah?"

They met the innuendo with grins. He asked what she paid. She told him. He told her he could make a deal happen in her favor if she didn't mind going with a two-year leased/pre-owned and Lynn said she was fine with that.

He said, "I'll make some calls. I usually have a standing game on Mondays, but do you ever play on Wednesdays?"

"I'm free. I could."

Got him. Now how does he get me to Elmin in the embassy?

"You up for doubles?" Aydin.

"Why?"

Son of a son-of-a, he's blushing.

"That shake-your-ass on the court. The pussyfooty—"

"Footsie?"

"—under the table. Yeeesss. Pretty much in my face with it all morning. So now it's my turn to make a pass at you. I have a cousin."

Lynn dropped her face—like dropping a glass not on accident, but to get attention.

He touched her arm. "He doesn't talk like you and me. He has manners. It would embarrass him, but I think you're acting naughty with me because you embarrassed yourself and—"

"Why's he single? He married?"

"You are so suspicious. No. He's single, and he's a catch."

"But you have a catch."

"I do. And it's going to sound weird."

"Yep. Just by saying it, the weird meter went way-way up."

"His job is particular about foreigners he can meet."

There it is...

"There's only one foreigner in this conversation, my friend, and I'm afraid it's not me."

"Come on. I'm serious. You two'd be good. He works at our embassy."

Elmin's his cousin.

"Sounds exotic."

"As if. No. Nothing like that. As I hear it, he's a glorified executive assistant." He rushed this next: "So, I would need your info first. Before you met."

"Definitely weird. But." She gave him back that first look of his, over the glasses style, and— "Tell you what, you'll want my info for a car, anyway..."

Lynn pulled out her driver's license. The one for *Layla Kingsbury.* "This be okay?"

"Sure. Great. Mind if I take a picture?"

"You can't memorize it?"

"Layla, you're funny."

Out with his phone. In with the pic. Lynn grabbed his device from his hand. Extended the length of her arm. Cheeked up next to him.

"Strike a pose," she said.

"Vogue it, girlfriend."

Selfie-snap. She got him to send it to her device which, in the subtle Agency way, while he was saying— "Did I tell you how sexy your voice is?" And Lynn was answering, "Good. It's new—" she entered a quick series of commands that once their devices linked, her phone wouldn't allow his transfer port to close.

3.

THEY WERE HUSTLING OUT through the kitchen to make early bell—Melody and the twins—and all she wanted to do was get in the truck, get to St. Pancras, and get on with the mission rat-gnawing a big hole in her stomach. Hal's schedule was later this week, so he was enjoying his coffee. The girls were there munching cereal and reading their phones—cereal boxes long-ago having lost breakfast-table attention. Gwen was on a later clock herself, dressed more conservatively than normal—at the round mirror in the dining room toning *down* her makeup—so something was brewing with her beyond her ongoing fight with Hal. Silas was on the porch reading the *Post*.

"Gwen." Hal answered one of her cracks. "I'm not talking to you about him. Period. Done."

"You refuse because you know he's alive—"

"I said, 'I'm done.' Done is done: Is. Done!"

"You're covering your own butt because you lied. On government statement documents: you lied. You're a liar, just like your sister."

Melody ducked her head and pushed the boys through to the porch. "Bye everyone."

Gwen: "Silas: you're the one who could fix this!"

"You involve me, someone is going to get into *real* trouble, and they might not share biology with me."

Gwen shoved her makeup into her bag. "You're all batshit crazy!"

Melody winced as she reached the door. Little Silas asked, "Do bats have crazy poop?"

Gwen wedged between them. Slammed outside.

"It's a Halloween thing, buddy," Hal called from the kitchen. Swiped at the girls, who giggled. "Bat *ship*. Like a pirate ship for bats."

"I want one of those on my next Jack-o'-lantern." Jack.

"I want a bat going poop." Little Silas.

"What 'next' Jack-o'-lanterns?" Melody—not finding her keys.

Charlotte didn't look from her phone. Her fingers didn't stop. "Mom left without us."

Melody centered. Found her keys in her other hand. Said, "I always take you."

"But she stayed late, so we wouldn't have to be there for the early bell."

"I can take you." Silas. "Or Paige, when she gets up."

Charlotte: "If she gets up."

"We're going to miss the early bell, anyway. Come on, girls. I'll wait." They bussed their bowls. "And what is this about more pumpkins? Are you sure, Silas?"

"Big house. Big porch. Like the olden days."

"Don't want to risk a fire," said Melody.

She caught Hal's eyes.

Oh, yeah. Doris. The fire.

Leigh. Sweater buttoned. Backpack ready. "Grandma Doris says she wants more."

Flat. An assertion. Hangs on the breath of the house.

"They're he-ere." Hal singsong'd *Poltergeist*.

Charlotte croaked, "Danny doesn't live here anymore, Mrs. Torrrrr-ance."

Leigh dropped her backpack, beaming. "Char that's it! That's what we can be—I'll be Danny! You be the mom!"

Leigh's eyes bounced from her sister to all the adults. Hal shrugged at Melody. Silas said he could only guess whose good idea it was to let Leigh watch *The Shining* and Melody pushed outside— "Come on, y'all." And over her shoulder— "I'll get more pumpkins. We're going to have the spookiest Halloween ever. Without scary movies."

The kids unloaded at the Academy. Sprinted the steep stone stairs to the St. Pancras bastion walls. Melody headed for town.

After the crime—awful/foolish.

Before the promise—foolish/awful.

Before Hal.

Before Silas became her true father.

Post bail/pre-trial. "It's simple, Mel. I'll 'no-contest' the plea. I'll take my time on this. But when I come out, you will have gathered for me everything needed to ruin Silas Kingston. To paint that oh-so-patriotic American family in racist shame for the evils they've hidden, the lives they crushed to feed their tobacco greed and grow their gold; I will see that horror-house brought down brick by rotten, racist brick."

"Destroying a family through their history—"

"Race crimes never go away. Double that for slavery and murder. America's itching for reparations. They ain't gonna get that, so they'll take their vengeance in

fire. Mark my words: race is going to burn this country down. Black people are angry."

"I'm not angry."

"You're in between. Can play both sides as it suits you."

"You're despicable."

"All they need is a spark. You'll marry that jughead—"

"I love him. I'm done with you. I won't do this."

"And you will *get me what I need to ignite the fire."*

"You drank too much of your poison. You're insane. You destroy the Kingstons—what do you get? Nothing."

"Nothing for me. Total ruin for them. Or...?" He licks his lips. Hankers for a drop of spirits of turpentine. Mixed with anything. "For one—make it an even three. Na. Five *million dollars. For five million dollars, I keep my mouth shut. My silence is expensive, but I can be bought. You're my proof to him—to all of them—of that. They're going to love you by the time I'm free. You're gonna have babies. You're gonna be the 'Kingston' Kingstons-can't-live-without."*

Melody looked at her wedding/engagement ring. Melody wasn't a two-band woman. The stone. A diamond. Less than a karat. Less than half. But Hal had told her it was perfect in every category.

"Like you."

With this ring: I am Kingston.

"There's a gun in a bag. Five bullets and a sixth empty shell in its cylinder. Got your mama and your name on 'em. Got your little tyke fingerprints. You know it's true. You'll tell 'em when I ask you. Long as I'm alive, no one can find that Ziploc baggie but me. I know you'll do whatever I ask. Do it right, I walk off with my money, and poof, I'm gone for good."

She kissed the stone. She let her eyes run. She swung the big wheel of the big truck into the tight and tidy parking lot for the Patuxent Historical Society.

👑 👑 👑

DIFFICULTY BREATHING. Muscle spasms. Sudden death. Except for the fleshy part of the red berries, everything else about the yew tree is deadly to humans. Ghosts dangled, strangled, from the branches of this ancient yew rising from the brown-faded lawn of the former Colonel Vickery House, now the Patuxent Historical Society building. Mica sheened the surface of the flag-stones Melody followed through rows of plastic grave markers with silly *Pardon Me For Not Rising*/*I Told You I Was Sick* sayings. Skeletons drank tea at a black iron table.

The spiders dotting the fake spiderweb over the porch-front holly were plastic, though Melody's step faltered as the polyester fiber quivered and thumped unnaturally. She didn't want to see what caused this, but small creatures don't distinguish between real and false deathtraps.

She peered gingerly over the top of the bush. Recoiled at the thrashing head of a snake, only to recalibrate and realize the "eyes" she'd seen peering back at her, were the brown/black patterns on dust-flying torn and beating wings. Legs jerking spasmodically on the reddish, worm-like torso of a giant cecropia moth. A rush of pity. Past the point of survival. It wouldn't live if she freed it, but she couldn't let the creature torture itself to death.

Uhhh, I can't touch that.

Melody reached in.

Jesus! It's the size of my hand!

Little fight left, it offered no resistance as Melody untangled it.

"There you—"

The giant moth burst into her face, and her "—*Go!*" became a startled shriek.

From the door above— "What are you doing?! Can I help you?"

An I-might-as-well-be middle-aged woman dressed in a rough faux-wool pantsuit, swear-to-god same colors and pattern of the moth's wings, held her in a befuddled look. Shook her head like, *Why aren't you answering me?*

Melody's fingers fluttered and twitched, searching her hair. "I'm sorry. There was... Forget it."

She mounted the steps. Approached the door. The woman didn't retreat to allow her inside.

Melody pointed at the wall plaque. "You're open. Right?"

Her nametag read *Victoria.* Victoria stood her ground. "Happy Halloween. How may we help you?"

Melody crept a hand to her hair. Made certain she was alone. "Happy Halloween. I love your decorations. I'd like to look at—access—documents you might have, the records, for slavery."

Victoria widened her eyes in challenge.

Victoria, this isn't your house.

But all Melody said was, "I'm looking for something specific. Local history. From back in 1698, when it be-gan, I guess through the Civil War. May I come in?"

And there I go, making it sound like it is her house.

"The public library would be much better for an overall history of slavery in Maryland. We have private documents, specific court and legal records, estate libraries and archives. CSM Leonardtown Campus has an excellent library—"

"Sorry to interrupt, but I believe you have what I want. It's a local farm—uh, plantation. Foxtail Farm? The Kingston family property."

Victoria's step forward caused Melody to step backwards. Caused the door to shut behind Victoria's rear end. Bump it. Like *Thata girl.* Like she and the house were in cahoots.

"You are correct. We do maintain their archives. May I ask—are you attached to a college or university? A historical society or research institution?"

"The plaque does say, 'Public Welcome.'"

"—or a newspaper or journalistic outlet?"

Poor woman looks constipated.

Melody allowed that to amuse her. It helped her gather a smile. Find her most gentle voice. "I've made you uncomfortable. I'm not—whatever you think I am. I'm not, and this isn't. I have a credential that covers what you're looking for with me."

There comes a point in an unspoken conversation where the cat gets your tongue. Where the things you didn't say have talked you into a corner. At least, that's why Victoria shut her yap.

Melody opened her purse. "I do hope you see the humor in this." About the same time Lynn was showing a fake at the tennis club, Melody produced her real driver's license.

"I'm Melody Kingston." Points out the address. "I live at Foxtail Farm."

Victoria's hand moved so quickly and furtively behind her it might have appeared—had Melody not caught it herself—Colonel Vickery, who many Saturdays in time-lost autumns, rode his horse to Foxtail Farm to share jug whisky with Silas Kingston III; to watch the negros box, and sometimes watch the former Silas box the negros—as if old Colonel Vickery had opened the door for Melody himself.

"We might have saved ourselves some confusion." Victoria gestured Melody Kingston enter past. Gestured again. "That's the reading room. Please wait in there. No food or drink. If you've brought writing material, you may make notes. If you use your camera, don't use the flash. These are gloves we'd like you to wear while handling the documents. It will be more than a few minutes to complete your request."

"Thank you."

Melody gave Victoria a chance to trade smiles. Victoria never took chances. She opened the reading room door.

"You're welcome. We close for lunch. But it's okay if you stay."

"It's nice of you to offer."

"There's a lot of Kingston material." A moment. Human. "Some of it is unpleasant."

WHITE COTTON GLOVES over golden tobacco hands.

Wooden ships.

Black iron chains.

A primer book: *Slavery in St. Mary's County, Maryland Colony.* Quick skim. Quick notes:

Number of enslaved Africans in Maryland explodes with construction of Foxtail Farm wharf. Before wharf: all of Maryland: 100 slaves. Ten years/wharf: 3,000.

By 1710, Foxtail Farm is landing between 180 to 250 African slaves. Per annum. For ninety-eight years. Stops 1808—import of African slaves outlawed.

Advent of the Civil War. Enslaved population, Maryland—includes American-born—over 85,000 individuals of the human race.

Something odd; something awful. Foxtail Farm Wharf specific:

1780 into 1830s. Discrepancies. The Kingstons pay out claims for slaves on manifests who don't survive the journey. Overboards/lost at sea.

More. Losses after arrival. Disappeared in transit. Wharf to slave market. From both—ship loss/transit loss—three percent yearly. For starters. After three years, leaps to ten percent. Runs consistent for a decade.

Losses ledger'd/initials *TJS.*

Always: *TJS.* Since the wharf's construction. Longer than any one man's lifetime.

Shipping cattle, shipping chickens, shipping hogs—that high a consistent loss was unheard of. But with human beings?

The Silas Kingstons, one after another, the offspring rolling their sleeves, pitching in: the blood money profit so high they didn't bother to reduce, prevent, or reverse this otherwise unacceptable loss.

Fucking disgusting human-vultures.

And (with this ring) I belong to them.

Boone Kelso had known how, whatever Melody found, it would hit her hard. But it wouldn't be enough to hold over the present-day Kingstons he'd connived for his daughter to join. He carried with him a name. A name given him by Doris Kingston. An Indian. Former slave of the first Silas. John Turkey. A slave hunter. Melody brought this knowledge, and she hunted him.

The horror story got teeth when Melody dug her way to the story of Turkey John Swann. Like the number of slaves to the colony, the accounts of this monster were plentiful and cruel, vicious and bloody. Newspapers. Public notices. Letters. Wanted bills marked *Rendered* and *Rendered Unto God.* Journal fragments. All pulled from various records, family accounts. Gathered like iron filings to a magnet dredged through dirt and cast into a single cash register-sized carton of unspeakable cruelty labeled *Kingston/T. J. Straw/Runaways.*

Melody quit reading the accounts after twenty. Quit tallying at forty and there were almost as many more to go after that. Turkey John Swann—

More honest if it read: *Serial Killer.*

A legally sanctioned serial killer turned loose by a grandfather of my own two children. Flesh of my flesh.

Someone, in more recent years—Doris, maybe—had listed the name of each runaway slave Turkey John Swann went after. A date of escape. A few bore crimes: *Larceny. Assault. Arson. Rape. Murder.* Most did not. All bore a date and resolution— *Rendered* or *Rendered Unto*

God. Specifics accompanied some, such as— *Lashed. Hanged. Beheaded. T&Q* with a handwritten margin note—

Doris?

The note: *Tortured? Quartered?* but most, Turkey John Swan would return with only a black and bloody scalp for the wronged slaveowner's satisfaction. Some whom he caught and returned—

The women—always the women and the children

—their names would inevitably make their way back onto the list later. Weeks. Months. Years. Turkey John Swann, always there in the end with tomahawk/without mercy. They too would *Render Unto God.* The final rendition. All ending in the same location: *Turkey's Swan Song.*

Her mind like a rabbit plunging tangled brush—

This place. This Swan Song. Where? What?

Kingston acreage. Excellent field for tobacco, but better used to plant the dead. A charnel pit with only a pretension of graves and makers.

Still there? (Must be. Somewhere.)

The next set of papers—

Must have been Doris who organized them; how odd it's Doris who's left me this trail?

—cemented the Turkey John Swan/serial killer conception in Melody's mind. They were construction orders, receipts for torture devices shipped from Spain, from Italy, for *"a place of blackness."* A number of accounts—she only needed to read a few—in which slave owners would bring their runaways, their recalcitrants, hand them over for *"Inward Light in the Place of Blackness."*

Torture.

Down the stairs.

Most hardened men who wielded the whip, white men considered the bravest of the colony, would take one look at the bloodstains, the gore, the wounded and dying already joined in the diabolical music of the instruments, barrels filled with the waste of unspeakable things and would step back. Their human chattel, dragged inside, screamed strange words. *"The water show us forth!"*

Melody did a quick back-flicking. Different pages/different accounts.

Weird. Most of them scream the same thing... "The water show us forth!" Here it is again, "The water show us forth!" And here—

She flipped forward into the accounts—richly detailed ones she would never allow herself to fully read. The same with every single one.

The water show us forth.

Melody considered this for a moment. Had to come from somewhere. Accessed her smartphone. Spoke. "Find Bible quote: 'The water show us forth.'"

Three hits.

"And God said, Let the waters bring forth abundantly the moving creature that hath life, and fowl that may fly above the earth in the open firmament of heaven." Genesis 1:20.

"Water will gush forth in the wilderness and streams in the desert. The burning sand will become a pool, the thirsty ground bubbling springs." Isaiah 35:6-7.

"On the last and greatest day of the festival, Jesus stood and said in a loud voice, 'Let anyone who is thirsty come

*to me and drink. Whoever believes in me, as Scripture has said, rivers of living water will flow from within them.'"*John 7:37.

All misses. Didn't help. And the strange, common plea—if it had anything to do with any of these verses—Jesus hadn't helped them one bit. The slaves brought to receive this heinous, unrighteous evil, this *Inward Light in the Place of Darkness*, never came out alive.

They departed in bloody sacks or coffins.

But for the grace of God, my mother's people. But for the grace of God...me. My children.

Her breathing ragged, hand shaking, she shut the file. Faced through blurring eyes, a last item. A page of diary foolscap. Not torn, but cut. Put aside for special attention. Melody lifted a Post-It note. One word in Doris's hand: *This?*

Beneath the sticky yellow scrap, written in crooked handwriting she would forever recognize as Turkey John Swann's:

"Nika swam today. Off the wharf. Before today's Guineaman arrives. My tomahawk was heavy in her hand. I worried she might lose it.

She is stronger than my worry. Arm and heart.

'The Lord Giveth' is the challenge and my brave daughter fresh-carved the parole. For history and purity.

Ever the song in our hearts. Truly, Nika is our melody. Her words will spread, and men will hear terror and laugh. Our Melody, my Nika, has learned eternal laughter lurks out of sight from man.

Vertigo struck. Melody felt the moth and batted at her hair.

Melody.

Her name clutched by and wedded to the hand of Turkey John Swann. A hand, his hand, thrusting from the depth of time to stab her with its quill. Splatter her with the blood dried into his ink. Her name to describe an evil child.

The flesh of his flesh.

A sob caught in her throat.

Kingston future. Kingston past.

Stumbled backward. Away from the mess of the table.

Bags of bones and blood and graves.

She ripped the white cotton gloves burning her hands. Threw them into the room. Pulled the door with her black hand. She fled.

♛ ♛ ♛

THE FIRST SHALL BE THE LAST. Gwen knew that from the Bible. People called. People chosen—law firms, for instance. Anything from the Bible was good luck. She didn't exactly know it, but Gwen sensed that was in there—the good luck thing—somewhere in the Bible.

God is all about good luck.

Her last appointment was the law firm she wanted. A firm steeped in intelligence cut-through-the-mys-to/hold-them-to-it/stick-'em-good work. Win every time. Marsh, Gertz, and Ossani. Only firm who asked for everything she already had for her case. Meeting set for 2:30 p.m., didn't hurt to get all her second opinions out of the way so she could sign on the dotted line by 3:00 p.m.

Gwen's last choice was first. 9:30 a.m. Fluffed her long black curls in the elevator. Lambert and Loeb. Went in. "We don't share your enthusiasm, Ms. Kingston." Came out.

10:45 a.m. Fluffed her long black curls in the elevator. Touched up her lipstick in the hallway. Nadir, Coleridge, Klein, and Dobrinsky. Went in. "Not the kind of case this firm can win." Came out.

12:03 p.m. Spritzed her curls in the car. Fluffed her long black curls in the elevator. Smacked her lips in the hall. Undid her top two buttons at the door—did one back. Went in. "Thank you for considering Garcia & Simon. Awful the way you've been treated. Wish we had the time to give this the full attention it needs."

Fuck your attention.

Out.

1:15 p.m. A rearview mirror wipe off the red, on with the cotton candy pink. Hair elevator and, alone, thumbed open the second button, a two-hand boob-push—nice "V"—in the metal-mirror doors. *Ding*. Reginald Mortensen, Legal Counsel on the door (quick perfume *pchit*). Went in. Mortensen is the nicest. Passes.

Makes a pass "Jerk yourself off, asshole." *Slam*.

2:15 p.m. Hair's fine. Wipes her lipstick. Likes it… Doesn't like it. Quick with a subdued red in the elevator. Curls *do* need a zinger of spritz. Fanciest door yet: Marsh, Gertz, and Ossani. The A-bomb of Intelligence Community law firms. This is the one. Turns the knob—

Shit. Top button. Prim and proper. In case we meet her today.

"Her," of course, was US Senator Theresa Ossani. Big Intelligence Committee who-ha. Went inside. Coffee. A Mr. Gertz handshake in the lobby— "No, I won't be in the meeting. I just wanted to tell you how sorry I am you're being put through this and your husband was, maybe is—hopefully, right? Beyond everything else you're dealing with— a patriot."

"Will Senator—" But he'd already checked-the-watch, white rabbit'd off.

Two junior partners. Long discussion. Deep interest. Real air of importance.

I like the gravi-toss. Better ask before we close...

"I'm assuming, due to her position on the Intelligence Commission, Senator Ossani will be deeply involved."

And the pause. The folded hands. And the placid/sympathetic smile like the best dump-drop in the world. "Yes. Of course. Understand, the senator is on leave of absence while she serves in Congress. She advises, but with a case like this where a conflict of interest might arise..."

Tag team. "Honestly, Ms. Kingston, *that* is the only reason we are unable to take your case, but what we would like to do is refer you..."

They might have recommended a firm she hadn't contacted who *would* take her case but swear-to-God her curls were wilting—she could feel them collapsing, dropping one by one—from the steam-heat bursting from her head. It was like being called Frieda again. From *Peanuts*, and Gwen is in Miss Othmar's classroom getting the *"Wah-wah wah-wah-wah-wah wah-waaah"* and—

I'll fucking call them back for the names! Put your back in it, hun—

SLAM! Good thing these were the best doors money can buy because only thick oak like this could withstand the heave-ho she gave them. Gwen felt marvelous. All of a split-second before, bosom-to-bosom, she collided with the distinguished Senator Theresa Ossani.

Gwen's finger, dancing like the Wicked Witch: "Some help all of you are! Thanks for nothing!"

Pulse unchanged, the senator stepped politely aside. Paused in the firm's lobby. Inquired of reception who Gwen was. Gwen Kingston. Not a Silas daughter. The daughter-in-law. The woman whose husband, the Deputy Director of Operations (her husband), Gary Gravin, was tangled with. The throat-slash sister. The missing (rogue?) officer.

Silas Kingston, the defendant. A way into OTRAC?

"Call downstairs' reception. I want Mrs. Kingston prevented from leaving this building."

4.

A BARN OWL, BOLD, swooped on Paige, startling her, wing-blasting her hair across her cheeks, before shrieking off.

In pursuit of Silas, Paige passed the center crossroads of the former agricultural portion of Foxtail Farm. Summer spent in a lovelorn stupor, unwilling to move life on from Clive. Her future unplanned, high school ambitions—press on to college pre-med, or maybe chillax trip to some exotic beach, or a cool job and an apartment and her own car—hollow and unwanted. Some great "Eighteen Summer." It all looked so immature. Empty of significance, which made it frightening.

Never having followed her grandfather this far before, coupled with the raptor's distraction, she lost sight of Silas, but a distinct notion that told her that his path veered into the overgrown, woodsy, southernmost section of the old tobacco fields carried her into the bramble.

Dark. Forbidding. Treacherous. Warned away and avoided in childhood, tonight Paige pushed through hanging cords of English ivy. Ducked beneath moonlight obscuring boughs of the tall trees sleeved by the evergreen creeper. An errant thought:

These twisting vines are like the coils of our lives, our once past, future come.

In this, she doesn't know she has already begun telling herself what Silas has lured her here to say. Her thought progresses as, adding to the ivy, she's forced to squirm through curtains of crossvine—the late summer bloom of their scarlet trumpet flowers, wilted, crinkled, and paper-dry, fall about her head and shoulders.

Alone, each vine's an unimpressive length of—what? Of monotony. Like a timeline extending, exact-same leaves at exact-same spacing. Going on. And on. Like monotonous infinity. Like summer. Like me. Like susceptible to one swift rip-it-down and done-gone-buh'bye. Only in their tangle/twists/strangulations do they become remarkable. Powerful. Overpowering, at times, lethal in the simple brutality of gathered mass.

Like family.

She grinned at her premise. Bright. The first fresh observation to perk her up from her summer lethargy. A tingle of bliss. Reawakened. Bright and blissful, and more startled by this than any devilish owl, she plunged deer-like deeper into the foliage. The forest shadows closed behind her, the vines linking like hands.

👑👑👑

EARLIER. Silver flash of the carving knife. Twins' glee. Pumpkins coming to life as leering—

"Jack-o'-lanterns—and it's high time you learn this, especially living here—"

"They're six, Dad. Let's not go too spooky."

"I want more spooky." Charlotte.

Leigh: "Me, *too-oo*."

"Melody?" Silas again. "It's your home now…"

"Fine with whatever." Faint/fake smile.

Adult eyes chained. Hal, Silas, Paige. No one re-marked; all of them, incorrectly, inkled a feminine condition. Not one of them in the kitchen—including Gwen who was not in the kitchen, who no one knew where she was (didn't miss her constant aggravation)—not even one of them could imagine Melody distressed because Melody never let another human see that side of her.

Melody stared at the knife in her husband's hand. How effortlessly it pierced and cut the flesh of the pumpkins. Sharp. Dangerous. Were they not pumpkins: lethal.

Silas cleared his throat. "Jack-o'-lanterns, carved with grotesque faces, are lit with fire to ward off the evil spirits of the dead who come on Halloween night—the ancient Celtic-age festival of Samhain—to steal the souls of—"

"Dad: don't say c-h-i-l—"

"—Children."

The girls laughed. The twins fake-screamed because Silas's spooky voice encouraged it even though—fascinated by their father's knife hacking out a jagged mouth—they'd not listened to their grandfather's words.

He murmured, "Children and anyone else they can get their skeletal fingers into." He crawled his fingertips across Leigh and Charlotte's, Jack and Little Silas's shoulders, their necks, *Ooooo*-ing like a ghost.

Went to the porch. The screen door. Pushed halfway. Stopped. He and Paige shared two glances. Interrogation and surrender.

He knows I've been following him.

Silas disappeared into the yellow glow of autumn moonlight. Invited her to the chase.

THE MOMENT THE IDEA she was lost crept up on Paige, a pair of angry yellow eyes blinked to life with fire. She forced herself through a high patch of lady ferns, finding, only moments before she didn't need it, the trampled path her grandfather made. It deposited her onto a wide, lumpy acreage. Hacked brush, dead kudzu, jutting roots, and piled thorny barberry, branches grooved and brown.

Its red fruit glistened like droplets of blood.

Half a football field away, Silas sat on an ancient stone bench beside his own Jack-o'-lantern carved from a warty goblin.

He made room for his granddaughter on the stone slab.

"You use that to carve that hideous thing?" She pointed at a machete between Silas and the pumpkin.

He grinned. Showed teeth. Patted the slab.

"How long did you know I've been following you?"

He mocked her with an obvious look.

"Why did you want me to follow you tonight?"

"Nights before, you needed exercise; cooped like a chicken all summer."

"Maybe I am chicken."

"Tonight, it's something we're going to test."

He patted the bench again and this time Paige sat. Looked out. The field. The woods she came through. "Aren't you like a king on your throne here? What is this place—this old bench?"

"A place fierce Jack-o'-lanterns like this one are necessary."

In the softest terms he could muster, he shared a brief history of the Silvanus Bench. Of Turkey's Swan Song. Of graves. Of bondage, of cruelty, of bones and the evil of his forebears. Because it was an evil—colossal and profound—where few soft words existed for it, his conversation was brief. It didn't matter to Paige; the horror and inhumanity even the smallest footnote that this Kingston history evoked was existentially so dreadful, Paige allowed it to pass her ears without permitting her mind to truly accept it.

The owl screeched. Another answered. The night breathed. Paige asked the question burning closest to her heart.

"Is Dad going to ever come home?"

"He is."

"Is his life in danger?"

"It is."

"Then how do you know, and can say it like that, like 'He is.' How do you *know*? Give me the details for eff-sake."

Raised eyebrow. "You know I can't."

"Not even here? In the middle of nowhere?"

"It's not the 'here.' It's not the 'middle,' and it's not the 'nowhere.' It's the you."

She told him instead. Paige knew about Turkey. Her father's arrest. His escape. "Uncle Hal fought to get him. Something crazy happened and Dad didn't want to come home. You've all—except Aunt Gwen—done this thing where you're saying he's dead."

The Jack-o'-lantern light flashed in Silas's eyes. Disturbed, but something else. Maybe a flicker of pride.

"C'mon, Papa. I hear the shouting. And I know Uncle Hal missed my birthday because you sent him again—"

"I never sent him—"

"Fine. Aunt Lynn. She sent him back. Somewhere else. Dad didn't want to come that time either. I want to know—not 'government secrets'—just why."

Silas shrugged. Like he would if she'd asked why the dog the twins hadn't gotten chased its tail. "He's on his own right now. Not with or working for the Agency."

"Doesn't that put him in danger? I mean, what about the airport on Fourth of July? That was definitely about Dad. They almost killed Aunt Linny."

"Newspaper said it was terrorists."

"I don't believe it."

Paige impressed Silas rather than surprised him. "Trusting your gut." Threw her a crumb. "The airport was your father's escape plan—which he made safely because he wasn't there."

"If he's on his own, what's he after?"

"His place. Where he fits in this family. How that relates to me and his mother."

"Was Grandma Doris a..."

"Spy? Of course not. Absolutely not. You're a lot like her, though."

"How's that?"

"Your curiosity."

"That's a good thing. Right?"

"The best. Maybe what I loved the most about her. Curiosity *and* her fearlessness."

"Will Clive come back?"

Of all of them, Silas understood Paige better than even his children. Her abrupt change of subject wasn't a change of subject at all for the way they communicated.

"Count on it."

"How do you know?"

"Fergus—the man he works under—Fergus can't catch me without him. With Clive, he's never been closer."

"How do you know?"

"As well as he supposes he knows me, I've known Fergus better for years. Always coming here and trying to trap me." Silas chuckled. "This time he thinks he will."

"Is he still around?"

An almost imperceptible shake of his head. "But he will be back. And Clive will fall in love with you again."

Don't say it. Don't say it. "Clive said you murdered a whole bunch of people. 'Good guys.'" *Dammit! Don't ask!* "Did you?"

"He says I did."

"Did you?!"

"Paige, I murdered no one. On our family's honor: never. I'll tell you this, though. Fergus is a nasty man. He'd murder me as soon as take another breath. He's the one Clive will have to watch out for."

"They're on the same side. You're the one who needs to watch out for them."

"That's not how I see this happening."

"You act like you know everything. But you can't see the future."

"I see the past. That's how come I can live the future backwards."

"Oh, yeah. Right. Like Merlin."

A sly smile. "Me, your dad, your Aunt Lynn—Hal, not so much; his job is all about living one moment ahead of the future—but us? It's like this. We envision what we want. Visualize/map out from that goal backwards all the steps that must transpire to get us there until we arrive at the bench you and I are sitting on right now. We watch them come real. A series of steps already taken in the past."

Paige wanted to understand but couldn't. It was okay. The lump in her throat told her it was okay. "I wish you loved Aunt Linny the way you love me."

The look Silas responded with promised nothing. "Get back to the house. And for the future: this is a private place, and you are never to come back here unless I bring you."

The meanness in his voice shoved her to her feet. "You did kill them. What Clive said."

"I know. You looked foolish pretending I didn't."

Paige stepped off and Silas—very much unlike him—snatched her hand. Held her fast. She turned. Wanted to wipe the pair of tears now upon her cheeks.

"Let go. What?"

Papa, don't ever let go.

"There will be a time when he comes to you and he asks you—or worse, doesn't—but you'll know. He'll want permission. At that time, you will do something for me."

"What?"

"Tell him this. It's from the White book, so you should remember it."

"*What?*"

"Tell him 'The bravest people are the ones who don't mind looking like cowards.'"

♕ ♕ ♕

A MAN, ANY MAN OR WOMAN, comes to a place where they cannot escape their past. That's hard enough. But a Kingston—this man on this cursed bench—a man of many pasts, fabricated, to be sure, but essential to those whom he connected with/connected to; essential to those whose presents and futures each one of his false pasts impacted in service of rules and circumstances, purely falsehoods, that engaged action for agendas across the lives of many people, all of them acted/reacted to each separate past, as fickle and transitory as Silas Kingston's plentied, disconnected set of lies: the man of many pasts resets after each mischief, but the damages those mischiefs caused, continue to thread. To tangle. Some to intersect and knot. And all these, wrapped in this: the multiplied, kaleidoscopic past Silas Kingston has tried and failed to leave behind.

Tuesday, October Thirtieth

1.

I N THE EARLIEST HOURS of the morning, Silas climbed inside the walls of Garde-Joyeuse. Not the Michael/Lynn orange stealing, Clive vaulting, garden wall. Inside the walls themselves. Narrowed by bookshelves of boxed loose notes and bound journals, twine-tied folios of antique papers, cylinder rolls and map-folded great sheets, the hidden, so unclaimed, life's work of the original owner of the estate—property carved out from Foxtail Farm by Silas Kingston III—Paul-Pierre Gallagher. He parlayed his early wealth from his investment in the Mohawk and Hudson Railroad into a fortune contracting with the Baltimore & Ohio to build the station houses, ahead of the tracks, one after the other, from Baltimore to Chicago. His life work, like the laying of railroad track, or better the leaves on Paige's ivy ropes, was a backwards identification and delineation of his ancestry which, at the time of his disappearance, he had graphed back to—or so he claimed—Jesus Christ's second cousin.

It was a massive genealogical library, these shelves which Silas moved between, a library that, since Gallagher's disappearance, only Kingstons knew existed. The hidden spaces between the walls and floor and foundation were a condition of the original sale and, although Gallagher was an architect and builder himself, Kingstons oversaw the engineering and construction of the mad rail baron's strange gothic pile.

Silas disconnected his microphones and cameras. He always did this before Fergus—and whatever whipping boy MI6 was keen on kicking to the curb by foisting them upon the poisonous Scotsman—arrived. He would allow a few days to pass, making sure he did not return until confident Fergus had swept and swept again and fooled himself into believing himself safe from counter-surveillance.

👑👑👑

MICHAEL KNEW NOTHING of the passages, the crawlspaces inside the walls of Garde-Joyeuse. Had no idea the original owner of the "haunted" house of the stolen oranges of his childhood traced his lineage to the second cousin of Jesus—which, if anyone bothered to open the boxes or unroll the calligraphied tree, would reveal the name of Timna, mother of Amalek (as traitorous an enemy as the Jewish people ever had)—and yet there was a kind of synchronicity, at least a similarity, in the unsealing of the boxes provided him by Kolya Yurenev; the shuffling through photo enlargements of CIA memos, plans, military manuals in English, and KGB reports, orders, and other ephemera written in Cyrillic, an alphabet Michael read well enough in quick skim to prove to himself their validity; a thorough timeline with enough corroborating evidence to prove Silas Kingston's bona fides as a CIA mole for the Soviet Union and a traitor against the United States of America.

Like anyone who consults the chart of the pseudo-hagiographer or the spy without order, without commission, without license and adrift of any law, the disruptor in the shadows, they would run their finger across and down the length and breadth to that primogenitor awaiting them at the bottom.

♛ ♛ ♛

SYNCHRONICITY?

On Silas's way out, the ladder inside the backstair wall, between the first and second floor of Garde-Joyeuse, he discovers a hatch. A kind of door he has never seen before. Within, discovers a kind of monastic cell.

A table. On it, ancient tomes. Greek, Biblical Hebrew, Latin, and Aramaic and Hebrew. Opened—face up, face down—or bookmarked closed, forming an arc around another discovery. The root of Jean-Paul Gallagher's lifelong quest. Two sheets of paper. Root cause of the strange man's death. Brittle dry and yellow. Insect-gnawed. A pen. An inkwell filled with a substance now like black sand.

A pistol on the floor.

A bone hand dangling above it connected to Silas's last discovery: the mystery of Jean-Paul Gallagher's disappearance solved; Silas's eyes track the skeleton arm to the shattered temple of its crumpled skull.

"This is odd." And Silas reads...

Michael examines a folder of surveillance photos. Not odd at all. Stomach-twinging-sad.

For Silas, this is the revelation that Gallagher's long-lost/discovered great-grandmother, Timna, mother of Amalek, the second cousin of Jesus Christ, Son of God, was also the sister of her own son. *Though Gallagher took it puritanically hard, this was not Timna's fault; the daughter of her father's concubine, she became his concubine. Ehhh...but she lived afterward as Eliphaz's (Jesus' uncle's) wife.*

Silas glowers at the skeleton. "What the hell'd you think it had to do with you?"

But, of course, it has everything to do with the dead man.

For Michael: these photos are of the many meetings/dates between his mother Doris and the older Russian spy, Kolya Yurenev, in and around Moscow. Kalaydoskop, the root of his lifetime of nightmares. Confusion.

Haunting, unshakable sadness.

Doris/Kolya: easy arms around accepting/inviting shoulders. Embraces. Kisses. Faces between each other's palms.

This shot: Doris's back is to the camera. Over her shoulder, Kolya makes mockery of it all, grinning directly into the observing lens. Big joke. Enormous fun. Bigger gut punch.

This has everything to do with Michael. It is not only eyes they share. Michael and Kolya Yurenev share the same face. It doesn't strike Michael as odd at all; he tells himself, let-me-tough-guy-through-it, Guess what they say is right—You marry a woman exactly like your mother.

Matched mirrors in a time tunnel. Synchronicity.

Timna and Doris. In both cases, a mother's corruption/betrayal of societal norms is the baptismal water at wellspring bottom. Live with it, or button your head with a bullet.

⚜ ⚜ ⚜

MICHAEL set the folder aside. There was one more thing he sought. The only thing he needed to know. The last and final box.

⚜ ⚜ ⚜

SILAS returns unseen to the North Vista Outhouse. Silas activates his laptop. Follows the instructions provided by Meryl Hofmyer that allow him direct access to Paige's desktop.

He clicks into her Facebook account. Finds the cover account British Intelligence maintains for Clive Lancer. Silas hopes he won't have to add this to the long list of forgiveness he begs of God.

He types and the kaleidoscope turns, heterogeneous bits and pieces, chunked from three Kingston generations. All of them converge from one pattern to the next. Dissimilar, but as always with catoptric instruments, in the trap of mirrors they hold symmetrical.

A TAPE RECORDER. Michael listened to the telephone call. Kalaydoskop from the Moscow Hospital/Silas from the mushroom lunch table in Yasnogorsk on the Vashana River outside of Tula.

"*Do you recognize this voice? Answer only 'Yes' or 'No.'*"

"*Yes.*"

"*From this moment on, you are to refer to me only as Kalaydoskop.*"

"*Yes.*"

"*The next voice you will identify. Only 'Yes' or 'No.'*"

Rough static. A panting, a whimper, a gut-deep cry of pain.

Michael recognized the voice inside the sob as his mother's.

"*Yes. You were her friend. She's practically a girl.*"

"*For someone trusted so well by your government in a position so important. They've put so much faith in you...and you put faith in me?*"

"*I put my highest faith in my wife.*"

"*No justice in that—our line of work or any other, I think.*"

"*Love is its own justice.*"

"*Should be its own justice, mmm? But, sadly, no. It is not. The least of justice lies in love. But we'll save that for another day. Perhaps the American cancer gets excised, and the world finds itself at peace. You are running out of time. Their lives for yours.*"

The accompanying report was five pages. Single-spaced. Dense paragraphs. Michael made notes as he laboriously worked through it.

Silas's cover as Lyle Pendry, Publications Procurement Officer, was compromised almost immediately with his arrival on station. His failures of his first year, the two assets he lost, all controlled by Yurenev who, as book critic, had ingratiated himself to Silas and his young wife.

Colonel Bogdon Ogievich of the Soviet Air Force Long Range Aviation: the dangle.

Silas took the bait.

Yurenev took his wife—

How long had he been taking her?

Doris's and Michael's life were the inducement. The duress/coercion followed. Silas needed to burn one of the West's own. It couldn't be CIA because that might lead back to Silas. Silas knew a British agent. An MI6 hotshot. Evander "Evan" Lott.

Lured into a trap. Kidnapped. Lubyanka. Silas handed the pistol. Cameras rolled. Lott's network rolled.

No turning back.

Seven Russian agents.

Chaos at the British Embassy.

Chaos with the Americans.

Two more British spies—their agents blown, arrested, executed—headed out of the Soviet Union. A car wreck. Two more MI6 killed.

Photos reveal a man known briefly to Michael as Pinwheel being taken into custody for running the traffic light. Disappears into a Soviet prison. With a revolving door.

Other photos of Pinwheel—

Dad's contact for the rest of his time in Moscow. The brush passes. The dead drops. The quick meets. All the early batches of American and Allied secrets before he, Mom, and I return to Foxtail Farm.

♛ ♛ ♛

Dr. Kiselyov offered to pull the medical bed from the room. Pull the guest bed out of the corner, out from the wall, back into the center. Michael didn't want it. As long as he was in the patient bed their relationship was doctor/patient. The faux-cherry guest bed, the linens, the blanket, the faded coverlet—too much private life attached. Intimacy attached. Or the sweat of loneliness for a dead/gone wife; the ponderous man wore a wedding band, but at no time had Michael heard another human inside the apartment.

Nothing about the doctor's hospitality/care said female. No. He wouldn't be this strange man's guest. He lay in the mobile medical bed and tried to sleep. But Michael's mind would not turn off.

What does Kalaydoskop want from me?

He hadn't found a single mention of the dual/dueling KALEIDOSCOPE/Kalaydoskop operations. No message conveyed by Kiselyov. No "Sophie's choice" inducement for Michael; NSA, no strings attached.

Before he opened the first box, Michael combed the room for surveillance. Nothing. He'd been allowed to go through it all, free and clear. The Aeroflot ticket and diplomatic pass. On the small table where the doctor left them. To take them. Free and clear. To leave.

Where is Kalaydoskop pointing me?

He wants me to believe, to know, he is my father. Whether Dad knows or doesn't know, he's undoubtedly always suspected. Maybe Doris told him. Maybe he's always known.

So what? So fucking what? All it is to me is a story.

The story of my cursed and fucking life.

He drifted off.

The jousting knights.

The red balloon.

"Give it back! The balloon man gave it to me!"

Lynn. Fist clenched. Seven years old. Screaming.

The beach. Michael running. Stolen kaleidoscope toy in his hand.

The wind moans over the treetops and Michael hurls it. Far. Into the Patuxent. From the past into the present.

Out of the patient's bed. Back to Kolya's boxes. Impatient. Pinwheel. His father's cutout. Set up—Geneva—to be his cutout. Wasn't supposed to die in Geneva.

Where does Kalaydoskop want me next? Pinwheel must have known.

Michael found the photograph. He woke the doctor in his bed. Fingers scrabble for the light. Picture shoved in his face.

"You know him!"

Dr. Dosifey Kiselyov shook sleep from his heavy skull. Squinted. "He brought the boxes. He was to come with a message for you if you asked. I was informed months ago he was killed."

"Is there a message? A number to call? A name? An address?"

"He introduced himself as Pinwheel. Said you would ask for him. But like I said—"

"The person who told you he was dead—"

"No one told me. It was a Swiss newspaper left in the lobby for me. No note. Nothing."

Michael's gaze fell to the photograph. His father, pushing a baby carriage, passing a small envelope to Pinwheel, who strollers the opposite direction.

"Me—the baby carriage?"

"That's when it was taken. I would assume, 'yes.'"

"And the baby carriage Pinwheel pushes?"

Kiselyov raised his thick and wrinkled eyelids. Eyes like olives, oily from their jar, staring. "I delivered a child for his wife three months after I delivered you."

He groaned. The bed groaned. Dr. Kiselyov rolled from it. Lumbered into the next room. An antique wooden cabinet of many drawers with a numeric code only the doctor knew. He knew the number he wanted. Pulled the long drawer from the case.

Scores of A5 cardstock, patient records. Photos of mothers and newborns. Without trouble, he found the card he wanted.

Stepped to his desk. A scratch pad. "Her name is Ludmila Sidorova. The father's name is not given, but he was present for the birth." Amused: "The way he chain-smoked, I am surprised he lived as long as he did."

If she's alive... Still in Moscow... Her father's failsafe?

"Could you help me find her?"

Dr. Kiselyov appeared to huddle into himself. "I prefer not to go any further with this."

But in the end, Kiselyov did, and Michael learned not everyone can be brave at all times and in all things. A person who rushes into every danger is foolish. But a truly brave person recognizes the angel upon his shoulder and goes beyond who they are usually at a time where circumstances are at their least beneficial to the brave man's survival.

Michael chose Moscow and a woman soon to change his life.

2.

F ALL CAME ALL AT once to London. A silent agreement between all the leaves, on all the branches, of all the trees. Skip the color kaleidoscope. Let go on three. Two. One. A brown, gray, dried out, dead slough-off the first week of October.

At least, that's how Clive saw it go down through his third-floor window at the Hotel Corbin.

Not that it was an easy window to see through; the glass hadn't known a sponge since it was puttied in place. When it had, the washers used the grease from their full English fry up instead of soap and water. Not much of a view. Even by Peckham standards.

A cracked wall, gated service/garbage area in the crook of the elbow-shaped building dominated by a London plane tree, its gray-beige-olive urban camo bark peeling in great scabs. A root had erupted through the driveway. Clive watched the walrus-faced owner have at it for two days with an ax and a case of dry Strongbow. Strongbow won; the squarehead whisker-faced, blubber-boy crushed his last can, abandoned the rubble, abandoned the splintered root, went inside and roared at his wife. A month after, the leather leaves all dropped at once.

There was the cleaning woman. A slight Bangladeshi maid. Did his laundry on Wednesdays. Cleaned the shower and the toilet on Saturdays. No prison had a more sparkly loo. Although she didn't clean the inside of his window, no prison had a better view. Although forbidden to speak to Clive, he knew the woman to possess a squeaky, ear-piercing soprano. One night, he caught one of his Minjerown minders dogging her upside the dumpster. Unsettling, that lady's voice, even in the throes of passion.

Beyond the dumpster, through the limbs of the trunk tree, he could watch a traffic intersection. The traffic lights improperly timed. Drivers don't tend to watch both at once. Most were used to it. But anyone new to the area, running late or right off the gun into the intersection, they'd learn the hard way.

The horns and squeals. The rent of plastic and metal. An every-few-day's and, more often, night's occurrence.

Turn up the television volume—that could drown it out. And while UK prisoners are denied television in their cells, Clive one-upped them there. His room had a new telly. Over 100 channels are available on a Freeview aerial. Wandsworth Prison got the same feed, but prisoners there had to argue over what they'd watch en bloc in the cell block commons. And Hotel Corbin *would* get a new aerial, would reacquire reception—just not while Clive was a guest in their keep.

In-room phone disconnected. Mobile device confiscated back in the States.

It was his rotating crew of four Minjerowns—two on/two off 24/7 across the hall—who were his only companions. That, and the running dog, yapping or gagging or shitting the hallway—but back to the vomitous/diarrhetic horror-show-in-mange in a minute.

His minders were under orders not to converse with Clive. Here's the length and breadth of conversation he got back from them the entirety of his incarceration:

"Don't talk."

"Step back from the door."

"You were told to mind your own business."

"Call it late tea. Call it early dinner. I don't give a fuck. There's one meal after lunch. Get used to it."

Note: Clive never got a "lunch." What he'd get would be a bag of crisps, or some naan dippers—mostly without dip—a lump of cheese, or a hard-boiled egg.

"Not listening."

"Time's up."

"Take it."

"Don't care."

"Can't hear you/don't want to."

"Weren't you told to mind your own business?"

"Over there."

"Tray gets left outside."

"We don't get paid to talk," which went right alongside, "You want what we do get paid for?"

"In you go."

"Finish your wank. Got church."

Oh, and the all-purpose, "Put a sock in it, cunt."

Back to "church." Though not church "church" per se. "Church" was a Minjerown euphemism for a prisoner outing.

Actual/in system/convicted prisoners, get a once in a while trip to court.

Equivalent for Clive? A session every ten/twelve days with his nameless interrogator/MI6 sorta-solicitor. Ol' Jolly Jack Ruddy Cheeks aka, in Clive's head, B-309C—the room at headquarters they always met. Church—as in confession.

Kafka-esque. Clive hadn't read any in school, but assigned enough Kafka over the years, and successfully cheated his way through it, knew enough to know hours on end, days and months running, questioned on and repeating, refining, what-if'ing the same empty details of the same few portions of empty hours he'd spent at the Foxtail Farm picnic table with Silas Kingston to no *If we get this, you get that* incentive/hope of any outcome, with no conclusion scheduled/promised/in fucking sight, was the esque-iest Kafka there was.

Kind of like a hypnotist, B-309C compelled Clive to recall the number of steps on the beach stairs. The strange mottos on the wharf pilings. The beads on Paige's birthday dress. The name of the cognac—Hennessy *Timeless.* All of it grasping at straws to erect a Little Pig's hut. Clive concluded the Big Bad Wolf of the whole damn deal was Fergus.

Whatever equivalent to Clive's imprisonment he'd been given wasn't enough, because, one Tuesday/Wednesday stroke of midnight, Fergus showed up. Comes barging into the Corbin. Hammered and hammering on Clive's door, calling for Clive's head on a pike.

Unwise, Clive answered the door.

Received a sock to the nose, but not a second one as Clive's Minjerowns beat Fergus. Tossed him out with a "Mind your own fucking business!"

Same as they said to the owner's inconsolable wife. Clive witnessed it out the window, by the dumpster, when the lady disposed of her awful dog. One or all four of his minders had obviously murdered it. "Peppy wouldn'a hurt no flea. This ain' right, no matter how much we bein' paid."

"It shit out its own guts. So mind your own business or you'll have something to cry about."

The shit smell went away toward the end of October, although the vomit aroma never abated and must have belonged equally to the husband, or the comings and goings of other guests Clive never heard nor saw.

Church: B-306C (Anton Hector—though Clive would never know that): "You're going back."

"Back where?"

"Foxtail Farm."

"Why? Did you uncover something?"

He slipped a print-out of a Facebook post across his desk. "You've been invited."

Clive took the page. Read the comment from Paige Kingston.

You're probably back at your university. You probably won't even see this or care. But I was wrong telling you to go. I want to say sorry. So "sorry." I'm so dumb, and my heart is broken because my feelings for you are bigger than any stupid b.s. my mom pulled. She explained. She apologized. And maybe I should move on, but I can't. I want you to know. I can't move on until you tell me you don't have any feelings for me—like you said you do. Because I can feel, writing this and looking at your profile pic, that you do. I think you do. I hope you do. I want you to SO MUCH. Because I really want a relationship with you, Clive Lancer, because (and don't throw up and don't let this ruin it) but I'm in love with you. I know I am.

I was since the minute I saw you.

Please come back. When you can. I know you have school, but if you can. Say the word and I'll come there. I'm serious. If "no," don't answer. Don't say anything. You can forget me. But I never will.

This followed by a second comment timestamped a minute-thirty-eight later:

*Never will *forget you. =-) Come fix my heart. I'll be nice. =-)) Promise. =-)))*

♕ ♕ ♕

EVERYTHING IMPROVED. All at once. Lunch became lunch. The Bangladeshi chambermaid thanked Clive for never reporting her trash-can tryst. (He didn't have anyone to report it to but, at least, they'd shared a moment they couldn't talk about.) One of the Minjerowns engaged him in conversation— "Wanted to tip my hat for giving us a reason to ass-kick your partner."

"Least I could do and, believe me, I'd arrange it for you to do again."

"Mind your own business. You don't arrange anything." He winked.

His last trip to church, Clive received the full briefing on Silas Kingston.

On Moscow, 1971.

On Evander Lott—including that Evan was Fergus's brother, and both Fergus and Evan's father were held in fond regard and high esteem by Her Majesty. A wartime connection, you see.

But there was more fueling the Queen's personal animosity against Silas Kingston. His involvement in the Wilson Plot. The accusations that her long-ago Prime Minister, Harold Wilson, was a Moscow spy. It wreaked havoc on British government. Tore apart MI5. Complicated relations with the American cousins and severely dampened (like having a bully hold your head in a toilet) US/UK relations during the most difficult period of the Cold War through the 1970s and '80s. Still caused problems. And who lit the fuse to that stink bomb? Silas Kingston who coordinated the smear for his CIA mentor James Jesus Angleton and their Soviet defector Anatoliy Golitsyn.

"Lott and his unfortunate murder— Ever-remains a nameless/faceless shadow. But the former PM that's public. That's a stain on our government and continues a scab disgruntled ex-spooks and over-zealous journalists keep picking at. The Crown wants it removed. Once and for all. The blame taken off the Security Service and the former Prime Minister's name and put where it belongs. Bullseye on the CIA and their own Soviet mole."

Anton Hector reinforced the importance of this on Clive on their drive to his Heathrow flight. "Whatever is proven on the one, triggers a decision on Silas Kingston CIA won't appreciate."

"Better Kingston than me." Clive caught a grin from the Minjerown doing to the driving.

"If we can publicly embarrass the Americans on their political interference vis-à-vis the Wilson Plot, we believe they'll give us Silas Kingston."

"I don't want to sink my own boat, but how's my affair with the granddaughter get you any closer?"

Hector stared at him with unmoving eyes. "The love note wasn't the thing that saved you. That was merely icing on the cake."

"What's the cake?"

"Find the cognac. The bottle is the Holy Grail of this whole bloody mess."

Anton Hector stared after Clive until the terminal doors swallowed him whole.

"Kid shouldn't be in this business." The Minjerown. (Even abusing Clive, he'd always liked the dumb kid.)

Anton met the minder's sunglassed eyes in the rearview. "No, he shouldn't."

Anton Hector didn't say it, not here and not to anyone over this protracted summer that had collapsed into a misty fall. But never once in his debriefing/analysis/investigation did Clive Lancer say he wasn't in love with Paige Kingston. Meant he was. Anton Hector found in his sixteen years at the job, it's the thing a subject never says, anytime he's given the chance, that is his truest statement of all.

The whole thing was going to prove bad. No doubt. But he liked the young man, too—an honest affection—so he hoped for Clive somehow, some way in this ugly, dangerous trap he'd worked his whole life to fall into, Clive would find one minute of total, carefree happiness. Maybe he would.

All Anton Hector knew for sure? For the first time working as an "anonymous" all three had agreed to the same result and had shared it with one another. Three out of three: at the end of this whole mess, there would be a termination with extreme prejudice.

Wednesday, October Thirty-first – Halloween

1.

THEY DON'T SELL TOMAHAWKS at walk-right-in Alabama off-price department stores. The Marshalls where the Alabama State Bureau of Investigations arrested Boone Kelso trying to pass the counterfeit dresses Melody made for him. They didn't carry tomahawks.

Melody's heart pounds. She huddles in darkness. Amazed by her gutsiness. How a few fast lies, some confusion—how years of trust can blind—brought her this far.

The family will find out. They'll know. But Kingstons deal in death. Have forever. Live with it. Never pay. And Silas will protect her as she is protecting him.

Big sunglasses. Hat. Concealer, foundation, color corrector; she's known her whole life how to hide the melanin in her skin. And off-price department stores in Alabama—every single one of them—sell carving knives for cash.

Her breathing is too loud. Too gasped. Too ragged. But everything around her is breathing: the air-conditioner unit she crouches behind, the traffic on the busy street over the wall she climbed, the trees that loom over it and there's an owl—like at home—this one urging her on as her father comes out the kitchen door of his Alabama halfway house and down the old concrete steps.

Leans against the rail. He lights a match. The fire breathes. He lights a cigarette; he breathes smoke.

Wait till he turns his back... Please turn your back.

She grips the carving knife hard enough to make her fingers hurt. Sweat covers her. Soaks her clothes. She steadies her nerves, picturing Hal. Picturing her sons. The three of them grinning at her. Each boy clutching scary pumpkins; Hal clutching the wet carving knife, orange fibrous strands of pumpkin brains dangling from the blade across his fist.

"Say 'cheese!'"

"Cheese!"

A photo. A selfie with them. An airplane ticket already on her phone. All the lies she's ever told them tumbling out at once. Surprise, confusion—

"Your father? I can see why you said nothing—but tonight? Now?"

Tears without sobs, without emotion, just words, "I've asked no one for anything. I need to see him. I must."

Boone Kelso turns.

Now or never, Melody.

It's six steps. He turns at four. Their eyes meet. He's seen the flash in the moonlight. His arms/hands go for the block, but she has the momentum, and she's never had the guts before, but this time it's his guts the knife plunges into.

Out and in again and he won't fall, but he can't do anything with his hands, and she stabs and stabs. Blood gushes.

Black iron chains.

Manacled wrists.

"I hate you! I hate you!"

My hand, my wrist: the blood's smearing my make-up. My skin shines brown. Like the darker, dying bird-hands quivering around the knife—

Screeching, owl-like: "I hate you!"

I have buried to the handle—

"Mel. Sweet pea. Why?"

—in my mother's heart.

"Melody! Stop!"

Hal?

Gasping. Blinking.

Mama? Hal?

His hand shaking her shoulder.

"Hal?"

"Honey, you're soaking wet. You're all shaking. What were you dreaming?"

"What time is it?"

"It's barely four. Wow, are you shaking. Feel you."

"Hold me."

"C'mere."

Melody twisted backwards into her husband, so they fit like the folds of a fan. Snug.

Safe? Yes.

She breathed. She relaxed.

"It's okay. Keep breathing. Yeah. Like that."

"You're nice and warm."

Outside the window, the fall wind susurrated through the trees. Owls screeched. Melody stiffened; Hal held her more tightly. These weren't the hooting horned owls of the pines. These birds were the tobacco shed birds, these birds added harsh chitter to the cryptic conversation of the rustling whispers of the leaves. She released to the waning night a realization Foxtail Farm, sinister and steeped in horrors she now knew it held, might never feel safe again, but Hal—

So strong. So warm. So real and alive.

—would always make her safe. It wasn't Foxtail Farm. Possibly had never been. It was Hal who was Melody's safe place.

"What were you dreaming about?"

"It's Halloween. Nightmares." She breathed in his scent. "What do you expect?"

He kissed the nape of her neck. She snuggled closer. And as things go in the night, he rubbed at her from behind. She rubbed her bottom back. Nothing happened for him.

"I love you, Hal."

"I love you too."

"Keep holding me," she said, knowing that his failure-guilt—not just now with her, but everything with his brother—was the nightmare and it was eating him alive.

♛ ♛ ♛

Since meeting Aydin, Lynn filed her contact report and debriefed with her NR/FR division manager, Stephanie Malkinson. Talk about living your cover; Steph's enthusiasm for a Lynn meet with Elmin Hasanov, the guy keen on a date, a target no one had hit for three years: oh, how proud Bitch-Boss acted. Like Lynn just learned to tie her tennies. Three years, maybe eight/nine failed approaches; Lynn spends an hour as Layla Kingsbury with his cousin, and now's headed to play doubles and make it lead to singles off the court and into his life. Woman was pissed.

Lynn, having presented her cover identity, made sure Stephanie had cover in-depth/ready to go. Backstopped *that* with Gary at DDO level because she didn't trust Steph-phony wouldn't be equally as happy if Lynn tripped on her laces and fell on her face.

"I'm happy for you, Lynn." She could see it in Gary's face. "Assumed you'd fight this. I was wrong. I'm proud of you. I'll make sure you're backstopped on the whole thing. If you need the H&R office populated, you got that too. You'll clear any cyber-sweep, and the Kingsbury home address is in a gated/drive-in complex no one's going to get to it. If this prospect goes hot—there's something to this guy—we'll have you in and personal life with history waiting for you."

"Thanks, Gary."

He let his eyes show her he cared. More than he should care. Usually, Lynn would play into it because she wanted it. This time, her only focus was Elmin Hasanov.

In her head, as she drove Halloween, first thing in the morning, to the Rock Creek Tennis Club, she revised her target's profile. Elmin's trips into the Kalorama gay scene weren't about him. He wasn't out on leisure time. Those secret trips were about Aydin. The man was looking after his cousin. No approach is going to work when you're trying to pitch someone on personal business who clearly doesn't want to be found out. It's why they crashed-out with Elim. But this: married and hiding the fact, jonesing for a date. Man's a slam dunk for compromise.

Right out of the locker room, Lynn joined Aydin. He'd already got a fourth from the pro shop white board.

"Hi. I'm Cathy."

"Layla. I've seen you play. You're good."

"I try. I do love it."

"It's nice to meet you."

"We're going to have fun." Aydin. "Soon as Roman finishes changing his shoes. I don't know what's taking him."

Roman? What the F?

"Your cousin's Roman?"

"He's Azeri. Like me. Here he is, ladies, say 'hi' to my stud cousin, Roman Sayadov."

♔♔♔

BETWEEN LOVE/LOVE and fifteen serving love, Lynn, Aydin, and Roman knew that Roman's partner, Cathy, was divorced, had no kids, owned three nail salons. Between thirty serving love—*Pop!* Uhn! Lynn—

Missed. Fuck!

Plop, plop-plop.

—knew Cathy had a lethal serve, and Cathy didn't know whether she liked wine or the beach or dancing best.

"Maybe you should have run *her* numbers." Lynn to Aydin, crouched in ready.

"Maybe I picked Cathy from the board to show you off." This time, Aydin nailed his return, and they made their first points.

Roman gave Lynn a firecracker of a private smile at the next inanity his partner delivered—

"What's it you do, Lynn?"

Pop! Uhn! *Plop-pop!* "Ehh! I keep the IRS off people's ass—" *Pop! Pop!*— "Uhnn! And I'll take gin over wine any night of the week."

—a smile, warm but shy, sweet and melting. Aside to Aydin— "You do know he makes you look ugly."

Aydin grinned and *Pop!* Drove home another kill shot in his Nike Killshots. Lynn revised her target profile.

♕♕♕

THE THREE OF THEM outplayed Lynn, who helped Aydin to a decisive loss. Cathy said goodbye on the clay—had to check in on her employees—but hoped they'd all do it again. Eyes hard on Roman, who seemed genuinely happy about the idea.

He said, "But I'm a guest, so both of you—" Cathy/Lynn— "make sure Aydin invites me."

After that, Lynn skipped a shower so she could meet the guys outside the lockers.

Revise. Elmin's likely his boss—how the three of them intersect. This might work.

Showered and Canali'd up, Aydin appeared first.

"Sooooo...?" Lynn cooed.

"Two things." He made a 'drink' gesture. They made their way to the juice bar. "I'm going to need to play with you a lot more. You have potential to be better than her. You just need some extra time with me, girlfriend."

"And the other?"

He tilted his head one way. Tilted it the other way. His eyes never moved off hers. "He's going to ask Cathy out."

"You got to be shitting me."

Aydin winked. "He's going to ask for your number."

"He's got my number. He's got my everything."

"He didn't put your info through. He's a shy boy. Wishes he had but thought it would be rude if he didn't officially ask."

Good sign. Already breaking protocol.

They got into line. Aydin ordered for all three of them. Waiting, he said, "If you guys hit it off, maybe we could double date."

Lynn's eyebrow arched, skeptical.

"I have a thing going with Roman's boss. They'd hate it—" He noticed Roman looking around. Waved. "They'd hate it—"

"But we'd have fun." Lynn completed his sentence.

Roman joined them. Took his wheatgrass. "I hate this stuff." He gave her berry-acai an inquisitive look.

Lynn sipped. "It's all bad."

"Right. You're the gin girl."

Smiles like McConnaughey. My cheeks are freaking burning.

"I'm on a—kind of a workout kick these days. But thanks."

Aydin smirked.

I am going to make this work.

"Aydin says you work at the Azerbaijan embassy?"

"He tell you I'm a secretary?"

Lynn held back her smile. Halfway.

"He did." Roman frowned. "Thanks, Aydin. He's right though," and Roman's laugh flowed easy and confident.

He inquired more about Lynn's work and, because he was honestly interested, Lynn had to bullshit. She channeled her best Numbskull Nancy accountant, without the desperation, but far enough that she liked the sound of it and considered how much happier she would be as someone else.

She asked Roman about tonight. His what-are-you-up-to's about Halloween. If foreign embassies did anything holiday.

"The few families here with children always drop by. We do a little costume contest thing." He chuckled, imagining the kids. "I give out candy at my apartment. It's a cool tradition you have here. I like the little kids who do the original stuff. And seeing their parents all happy. It's a fun night. You?"

Aydin's head swiveled. Watched the conversation lob easy across the table.

"I did like that. Always. But where I am now, there aren't many kids."

Drop the bait into the water.

"Last few years, I leave out a bowl by the door. There's this place—"

Think fast.

"—Madam's Organ. Chicago-style blues bar. It's got like five bars-don't-mention-gin. They cut loose for Halloween. I used to live near Adams Morgan—"

Fuck. They're gonna have to add it to the legend. They better have an address.

"—I try to run into old friends there."

"You dress up?"

Sniffing the bait; doesn't see the hook.

"I got a halo and some skimpy little wings. What more do I need?"

Aydin wiggled eyebrows. Roman gave his Matthew M smile right at her. Wasn't blushing. Her eyes twinkled his and she pictured the fishing line dangling between his lips.

BETWEEN THE ROWS of Jack-o'-lanterns lining the porch steps, Melody used a darning needle and black yarn to sew a white felt rocket onto an old green sweater between two felt stars. Already stitched in black and running down the white were the letters N-A-S-A.

She sat on the third step and over to the right, unaware her mother-in-law Doris had always sat in the same spot. It was the last spot Doris ever sat outside, ten years ago.

Silas knew. He watched Melody creating Leigh's "Danny Torrance" costume, and she watched her sons chase each other on the lawn where Hal had caught his first football when he was not much older than Little Silas and Jack, yipping, hollering and clacking the blades of their wooden swords together with the desire to draw blood nonexistent in their innocent hearts. One wore a dragon-headed green cape, the other wore knights' armor of cardboard box sides spray-painted silver.

For an instant, it was Doris and not Melody; he'd caught her vainly trying to adjust her wig and while she could not smile that Halloween, so late in her life and so near its end...

Doris meets Silas's eyes. Smiles. Strikes a pose, hands presenting/mocking her wig; Doris kisses the air they once breathed between them.

Leigh watched Melody's every stitch. She said, "Did your mom make your costumes?"

"Until I was about your age."

"Did you buy them after that? Or did you make them? You're really good at it."

"Thank you. No. I didn't get to do Halloween, not with costumes, not after that."

"Why?"

Melody completed a stitch. Judged her work. She added a bind-off stitch and cut the yarn. "My dad was kind of a traveling salesman. We were always moving around."

"What about your mom?"

Melody stretched her lips in a flat, closed smile. Blinked.

Charlotte, having come out behind her, knew the answer. "Leigh, remember? Her mom died when she was a kid."

Leigh's cheeks paled. She looked at her shoes. Melody lifted the child's chin.

"Hey, bright eyes. Nothing like that's ever going to happen to *your* mom."

"What about you? I'd miss *you.*"

"Well, you got me forever. So, tough luck." She turned so Leigh couldn't see her own eyes bright with moisture. Said, "Charlotte, I don't know how you did it. You have every piece of the 'Wendy' costume."

Charlotte beamed. "The main piece—this ugly brown overall dress—it must've been Aunt Linny's. It's the wrong brown, but it was in one of those chests."

"No, it's perfect. And Uncle Hal's baseball bat. Great. What we're going to do on those big white paper bags—" The girls nodded, anticipating— "Is you're going to cut out letters and glue them on. On yours," she pointed at Leigh, "you're gonna do: H-E-R-E apostrophe—"

Leigh: "S!"

Charlotte: "And I do 'Johnny'! That's so cool, Aunt Melody!"

"I still say a better costume for the boys would be dresses," Silas chimed in. Got him three curled lips. "The evil twins! Ghosts in the elevator, you knuckleheads."

"Oh, yeah," and the girls giggled, and Melody said to Silas, "I didn't get my walk this morning. If you could watch the four of them..."

Silas gave her an up-down appraisal. "What's with the hiking boots? I usually see you in sandals."

Melody beat guilt from her expression by opening her mouth to a broad smile. Gave a funny eye roll. Made a kiss at him in the air.

The air between them stopped breathing.

My Doris. This night you died.

"Ah," he said. "Have at it."

♕♕♕

THE AIR HAD NOT MOVED since Melody set out from Foxtail Farm manor. She realized it now as she explored the unkempt land around where the old slave quarters once stood. Insects. Birds. Lizards and other creatures. Nothing moved. All unnaturally silent.

Maybe after noon it's always like this.

Maybe saying that to herself didn't convince her. Though the wind was still and the sun was warm, Melody's skin grew cold.

If there's some Swann Song graveyard, it won't be here—

A purring sound invaded the silence.

Not close to where they lived...

Her eyes lifted, her vision drawn to a free-standing, half-tumbled brick curing flue. The other side of the crossroad. Some of the ancient poles remained, broken and tumbled. The purring came from two of the juvenile barn owls strutting along a dry wooden beam.

They must have found a new roost. I better go.

They chittered. She couldn't take her eyes off them. She'd not walked that morning because of the mated pair.

Beyonce and Jay-Z. It's not even funny.

They'd perched on the railing of the widow's walk atop the North Vista Outhouse when she first came outside. The male and the female both spread massive wings. Made no other sound. Made no move to fly. Glittered their eyes, opening and closing their beaks, staring at her. She remembered, as she stared back at them, that the local tribes, the Piscataway—

Turkey John Swann

—believed owls harbingers of death. Sudden and soon. She'd started on the costumes. Tried to forget. Now, here she was.

Walk away. Don't look.

Two more juvenile barn owls purled from the brick chimney stack. Hopped on the blood-red manufactured stones. Clacked their beaks. The others clacked theirs. Somehow, now all six of them were there.

Leave. Be calm.

Melody made it three steps before the first of them struck her head, talons first, tangling in her curls. The bird's scream matched her own. Her hair tore from her head; the owl's beak pulled skin from her skull. Struck bone. Her hands went up. Grabbing. Hit away by furiously beating wings.

Stop it! Hurt it! Kill it!

That's when the second raptor slammed into her back. Stabbed and gripped. Pounded its beak. She ran, stumbling, dust billowing, into the force of two more flying directly into her chest and shoulder. She turned her face in time to avoid another set of talons aimed for her eyes. Screaming until she choked on feathers and dust. Blood spilled down the back of her neck. Her forehead. Her cheeks and into her ears.

A powerful force wrenched her arms. Gripped her wrists. Spun her violently across the road. The owls leapt for the air. A gunshot exploded the air above Melody's bloody head. Another explosion of gunpowder and shot.

Silas threw his shotgun and gathered her. Easily, light, protective, as if she were a child. With Melody bleeding in his arms, he ran.

2.

S ILAS AND MELODY RETURNED from the hospital to Foxtail Farm, the entire back of Melody's head shaved and stitched. Her cheek and forehead: stitched. Her forearms wrapped in gauze. The backs of both her hands wore large adhesive dressings. Beneath her sweater blouse—stitched shoulders, breasts, and back.

Charlotte said, "The twins both fell asleep."

And Leigh followed with, "They're both really worried we're not going trick-or-treating."

Exhausted. Whirring on pain pills. "I'm going to lie down. Just a little. For myself. When they wake, you tell them, of course we're going to go. And Silas—or Charlotte, better. At three, take the slow cooker big dish out of the refrigerator. Put it in the slow cooker. And set it on high for three hours. I made pumpkin chili." She started off the porch into the dining room. Noticed Doris, watching her.

Don't worry. I'm okay. I am.

The pair of them mirrored. Stopped. Turned back. "Tell Hal not to wake me. Not to come up. I'll talk to him when I come down."

Hal, off early, was home by 3:30 p.m. He whispered with his father. He comforted his boys. He couldn't get his own from the bedroom, so he borrowed Silas's shotgun.

Went out to the curing flue. The juvenile barn owls had moved into it and nested. Hal shoved in tinder. He lit it.

When the remaining sleeping birds spooked and flew, he killed them on the wing. One after the other.

AFTER THE HORROR of the day, after the comfort of Melody's Halloween chili, Silas begged off trick-or-treating. Gwen was AWOL, but Silas somehow knew why.

"She's lawyered up. Been meeting all day with Marsh, Gertz, and Ossani."

"Isn't that Senator Theresa Ossani's outfit? The Chairwoman of the Intel Committee. Fuckin' bitch." Hal was pissed. Pissed all summer.

"One and the same. It's illegal for that harridan to be practicing while in Congress. Then again, it's against the rules for her to be married to the DDO, but no one seems to care about rules in government, not much anymore. So she 'consults.' You'll be hearing from them, hoot-owling at your future. I imagine."

Melody—as she said at dinner, "I'm the rag doll from the Tim Burton movie," didn't need a costume—she and Hal squeezed the four children into her bad-ass Billy Goats Gruff Ram and rolled into the old town where the square, the shops, the historic homes on all four sides, and the houses two blocks deep, each became a frenzy. Parents and scary/fantastic/oh-aren't-they-cute children, door-to-dooring it from 6:30 p.m. to 9:00; sugar and hormone hopped teens rolling in around 8:00 to grab some sweets, show off, chase and flirt and silly-string and smoke bomb and maybe get a little sugar from the opposite sex, but mainly to hang out, slung and slow and cool in the silver moonlight of the center park where the local cover band, Firestone—always off from/sponsored by Clancy's Crab Broil on Halloween—once a year changed their name to Fire-N-Brimstone and rocked the night for free. House parties—the young single married crowd and the old money crowd clatched and klatched; did everything from flaming-shot "grave"-yard parties to cigars and spirits and lawn chairs plastering themselves into undead.

The twins were adorable. The Questing Beast, Glatisant, and the Saracen knight, Palamedes, who took over the chase of the dragon when love waylaid King Pellinore. No one who asked knew what the hell they were talking about. Melody was told, one hundred times or more, she had the most realistic makeup any had ever seen. Until they realized it wasn't. Word spread. Children's eyes shielded. Dirty looks abounded.

"Have you noticed people aren't too sympathetic on Halloween?" Melody quipped to Hal as she tilted her head at two passing teenagers—like a broke-neck girl—shoved out her tongue. Pain pills whirred. Hal didn't notice. He was still pissed off. If anything, was brewing to strange fury.

Charlotte and Leigh, equal parts awesome and age inappropriate, won the costume contest on the stage while Fire-N-Brimstone took a break after a rousing *Monster Mash* to arrange music stands for their brass and reeds backup as they prepared the adult portion, Oingo-Boingo performance. Melody allowed the girls free rein to stay, for the concert and other mischief on the green. She, Hal and the twins—a single family unit for the first time this Halloween—traipsed back into the neighborhood. A few more candy-handful haunted houses because it's only once a year. Hal led deep into the neighborhood. Wasn't open to suggestion.

"These streets are maybe too dark." Melody.

Silence, Hal.

Still, the porch-posted witches and crazy clown cowboys were generous (and horrified by Melody); the four of them were coming along a path to a cobwebbed fence when two things happened at once.

"Oh, sheeze! Mrs. Kingston, what happened to you?!" Victoria—from the Colonel Vickery House—whose Victorian vampire makeup didn't look any different from her day-to-day brush-up, blocked their way coming through the arbor arched gate.

"I-I—Victoria—" She didn't have any children with her. "It's a long, bizarre story. Why are *you* here?"

"This is my parent's house. I live here. How do you do, Mr. Kingston?"

"Yeah." Hal's eyes were roving. Saw something he didn't like.

"I wanted to call you—" tentative, "—Melody."

"I'm sorry, I left it so—"

"No. *That's* okay. I found something you need to see."

"That's great." Hal butted between them. Ignored Jack and Little Silas hop-footing around their legs.

He placed both his hands on Victoria's shoulders. "Listen to me and don't ask questions. Take my family into your house. They aren't in any danger. No one is. But there are some people I need to lead away from us. I can't tell you anything else. You understand?"

With a guy like Hal, a pro at giving orders under fire, expecting and knowing they will be carried out, Victoria's reaction was one she never expected to give a stranger.

"Absolutely, sir."

Two foot-teams and a tail car had been rotating around them for over an hour. Hal's family went inside the house (to the confused delight of Victoria's parents; had their Victoria made a friend?) while Hal—when none were looking—slid his holster from the small of his back, clipped it to his right hip and took off at a quick I-dare-you stroll.

♛ ♛ ♛

PAIGE CAME DOWNSTAIRS to the dining room after she heard Melody's truck drive out. She waited in dim light at Doris's round table, swaying as she played with the optical illusion of Doris appearing right over her shoulder in the curved surface of the Witch's Eye mirror. Debated whether to make her call first and then tell Papa, not tell him at all, or tell him first. She was tapping her phone in her hand, looking at Doris, looking at her, when Silas answered the question for her.

He left the North Vista Outhouse at a quick pace to his car. He drove a little faster than usual out the gate.

Paige dialed the local taxi service.

♛ ♛ ♛

IT WAS 9:15 P.M. at Madame Organ's, where Lynn was drinking club soda with a wedge of lime from the bar gun. Lynn tipped five bucks a pop on it and received excellent service. An extra five spot ever thirty minutes kept the stool beside free for her purse—even after making it clear to the bartender when he said— "I sure don't mind saying it, but you got some devilish voice for an angel."

"My niece says, 'I'm drawn that way.' Look, you'd be right for me a dozen different ways, a dozen different nights, but tonight I'm waiting on a date."

Not two minutes later, Roman Sayadov asked if she wouldn't mind moving her purse.

♛ ♛ ♛

BEFORE DRIVING AWAY from Foxtail Farm, Silas had been on his roof. From the North Vista Outhouse widow's walk, looking away from Foxtail Farm, looking to the Patuxent River, the single-mast skipjack oyster dredger appeared and anchored with the rising of a gibbous moon. It was not the same boat that bobbed and lingered that other Halloween season. Couldn't have been. Silas burned that one to its hull in its slip the night of Doris's burial. This time, he signaled the boat. An infrared beacon.

Two if by sea.

He didn't need a response. Knew he wouldn't get one. And now, he drove his big-as-a-boat Cadillac Brougham along the center of six faded lanes of cracked, pot-holed, weedy blacktop. The road bent through deep semi-wetland forest. He maneuvered past the last ruined parking kiosk. The junk-pile parking lot stood empty.

Silas walked beneath the worked iron letters of the crooked metal entry arch. *Enchanted Forest – Merlyn and Morgana Bid You Welcome!*

MERRY MUSIC SWELLS. Smells of cotton candy, popcorn, cookies, hot dogs, cakes. Costumed characters of Arthur's court swirl and dance. A juggler draws oohs and ahhs, tomahawk hatchets spinning safely between his hands. A maiden blows bubbles the size of deep sea mines that harmlessly pop and delight.

Doris pushes Lynn. Lynn is a bit too big to still be in her stroller. But she is contained.

Silas holds Michael's hand. Occupies himself with the fantasy that, if he lets go, the boy will surely bounce away into the streaming, happy crowd. But the amusement on Silas's face is pasted on false. Silas dreads his yearly meeting with his Soviet handler.

He dreads his handler handling his wife. As if he owns Doris. And Silas knows he won't stop him. Kolya knows this, too.

The cartridge of subminiature film in his pocket weighs as heavy as his steeled heart.

♔♔♔

TONIGHT, SILAS carried a North American Arms 22LR. A compact, five-shot revolver. Kind of a bullet, popped in right, rattles around before/if-it-ever pops out. He softly passed through the castle where the ghosts of the invented two children laugh at him and haunt. A shortcut through plaster and chicken wire and teenage trash. A stop at a spot only he and Kolya know. Out to the remnants of the princess carousel.

The cement pad next to Merlin's Kitchen. The twenty-foot stone-sculpted, green-eyed owl. In the embracing shadow of its half-opened wings, a pistol of his own: a man he's not laid eyes on in thirty-two years. The man who knows where his son is. Who manipulated him and held his life by the lure of the same blood running in Michael's and Kalaydoskop's veins—

Kolya Yurenev.

♔♔♔

HAL KEPT a steady pace. Around the corner. Down the lane, between garages and carports at the backs of the old houses. When the Asian man and his female companion entered the lane after him, Hal was nowhere to be seen. They increased vigilance as the woman spoke quietly into her earpiece mic.

Didn't finish her sentence as Hal tackled her from above, parried the series of blows thrown by her companion before slamming his head into a wall. He seized the dazed woman coming to her knees. Kneed her in the solar plexus and tossed her into a metal roll-down garage door before vaulting a backyard fence.

Hal came out, charging across the lawn into the pair of Caucasian males paralleling his original path on the next street. Drove one into the trunk of a blackgum. Whipped out his Sig-Sauer. Shoved it under the second man's jaw. "Keep your life. Talk."

A screech of brakes. A car's shadow cut the silver moonlight. In a single move, Hal was behind his captive, muzzle pressed into the base of his skull, his body shielding Hal from the vehicle.

"Hal Kingston."

"Got a lot a nerve, whoever you are. With my family around—? Fucker."

The rotund man pushed out of the sedan. "Morton Drexler. We've never met, but we could be brothers."

♕ ♕ ♕

A KNITTING NEEDLE plunged into the neck.

Final chase/last struggle. His own knife plunged into his chest.

Six gunshots.

A plunge from a balcony.

A look to the lawn below.

Michael Myers... Vanished.

Paige and Morgan released their breath as *Halloween* ended.

"Time for more popcorn. Put on the next one, lover." Morgan flung the sofa throw from their laps.

Lover? Weirdo.

Morgan grabbed the empty bowl. Made her way through the dark of her parent's empty house to the kitchen. Rustled around.

Paige called. "*Halloween Two* or *Chuckie?*"

The microwave latch. *Beep. Beep.* Keypad commands.

Paige twisted the lamp switch. Nothing happened.

Paige called. "Hey. The bulb burned out."

Morgan didn't answer. Paige used the light on her phone.

The microwave whined in the other room.

Paige searched the stack of waiting DVDs in front of the entertainment deck.

Popcorn popped.

She smirked at the cruel fat-cheeked doll with the flaming orange hair and oversized butcher knife. Cued up *Chuckie.*

Ding. The microwave.

Paige snuggled under the fleecy throw. Thirty seconds later, the microwave: *Ding-ding.* A "ready" reminder.

"Morgan!" Nothing. "Very funny... Morgan?"

A horn beeped out front. The front door shut. Heavy. Hard. Paige flung the blanket.

She ran to the front of the dark house. Threw open the door in time to see Morgan driving off in the passenger seat of her latest boyfriend's Mustang. Her arm trailed out the window. Waved. Her middle finger.

"Bitch."

Paige searched her sweatshirt pouch pocket. Remembered she used her phone searching the DVDs. Went back. The instant she stepped into the TV room, she noticed the sliding glass door was open.

"Hello?"

Okay. This isn't funny.

Right beside her ear: "Boo."

Paige screamed, spun, staggered back. She would have fallen had the man not grabbed her hands with both of his.

Paige's heart, already pounding, beat faster. Both said the other's name. Paige, incredulous. Clive Lancer with a big fat grin.

Both stopped waiting for the other to speak. The next thing on Paige's lips, on Clive's lips, were their lips.

"Morgan's parents are out of town."

"I know. She told me."

Paige snatched the blanket and led him to the stairs.

3.

S OME ANIMALS DWELL IN mimicry to thrive in their environment. For defense. For avoidance. For killing. For control of an otherwise disadvantageous food chain.

Batesian mimicry: in which the mimic appears as a familiar threat to be avoided rather than investigated/approached as prey.

Müllerian mimicry: two opposing adversarial creatures appear to each other as similar. Allied.

Aggressive mimicry: where the predator appears a harmless target to their prey. Lures them to their own destruction.

For these creatures, it is pure instinct. The giant cecropia moth, whose wings display the face of a snake; the spider-tailed, horned viper, who devours warblers the way you would guess: they so much could choose to display or behave otherwise as they could choose to read a book. Mimicry, in nature, is an evolutionary adaptation.

All spies, at some level, are naturally predisposed to mimicry; those who operate in the field, train to expertise. As such, it is a behavioral gadget in their field kit.

For Kolya Yurenev, his natural born ability for mimicry was more animalistic than human-trained; as a man gifted with reason, he could turn on or off any of the three kinds of zoological mimicry—defensive/ward off, deceptive/blend, destructive/lure in—at will. Could blend into any group he entered. Could lure as irresistible as a shiny penny on a sidewalk draws a child. He could present the most unattainable of desires suddenly offered from a warm and open hand, or be the worst of fears, monstrous and unmovable on a path, bending prey to his will.

They say the best of spies are all things to all people, whomever and whatever the situation demanded, this due perhaps to a personal flaw, the inability to be anything to themselves. Kolya Yurenev was all things to all people, in all moments. Upon having met him simultaneously, three people could easily come away from the same encounter one choosing to ignore him, one lured to his desire and their detriment, and the third never noticing, or if having engaged in conversation, having no memory of it at all. Kolya Yurenev could steal your wife's heart while enslaving your own heart utterly. He was a magnet to dreams and ambitions, desires and needs. When he wanted, he was invisible.

His physical display was much the same—hair, face, height, weight, and bearing—pleasingly generic. His appearance was what you wanted to see reflected back onto you. Or it was what he wanted you to see. Or you didn't see him at all.

Silas saw him originally and always, even after he knew it was illusion: professorial, gentlemanly, and warm. The way, Silas thought of Satan; even when you know him, the devil will always brush alongside you and share a smile. Doris and Michael, no matter what else they knew or rationalized, would forever feel a paternal aspect, even at the point he was destroying them, something Silas hoped Michael would deny were he to get the chance to commit patricide.

The moment of Michael's birth, when all three Kingston lives hung in the balance—no matter what choice Silas made—Kolya Yurenev had already taken their three hearts. Kalaydoskop would possess them forever. Kolya inspired trust and could consume it so fully that even when he broke it, you remained forever entrusted to him. He didn't share; what he inspired you to offer him, he took without mercy.

Mimicking both a father and grandfather to Silas's family, Kolya Yurenev was their cancer.

It was cancer on both Kolya's and Silas's minds this night, this anniversary of the Halloween their beloved Doris died, and their conversation moved inexorably toward her, mimicking the disease itself as the disease had mimicked a treatable infection until it metastasized in her lung.

"You planning on shooting me?"

"Silas, your right coat pocket is out of balance."

Silas waited. His face offered nothing.

Kolya turned his gun between his hands. "It won't bring her back."

Silas considered it. "Might get us all together again."

Kalaydoskop pocketed his weapon. "Security?"

"Tonight: clean. CI is probing. It's elliptical. For now."

"Drexler?" said Kolya.

"Made a run at my daughter. Now he's going at my other son."

"Why don't you do something about it? Him."

"'The devil you know...' as they say."

Michael—right where I stand. Red balloon. That crushed expression, crushing me forever.

"If you raise them right—" Silas's eyes stabbed— "you trust them. Implicitly."

"And if they make mistakes?"

"Especially when they make mistakes."

Kolya lowered himself to a rounded concrete bench. Leaned against the edge of its matched and broken table. "Do you have what we need for Baku?"

He gestured for Silas to sit at the next table over. Silas ignored the invitation/command. Said, "What are you doing with Michael?"

"Controlling a situation you have allowed too long to get out of hand. More than four decades."

"Michael is not and has never been your concern."

"He has always been my concern. It has always been leading to this."

Every muscle in Silas's body clenched. Include the muscle at the center of his chest. But he couldn't hold this back: "Is he safe?"

"For now. We have a situation with the Chinese."

"My read is Xi Jinping will assume leadership at their Twelfth National People's Congress in March. I believe, unlike Hu Jintao, Wànhuātǒng is Xi's priority."

Kolya assented with a dip of his chin. "Wànhuātǒng: their kaleidoscope. It almost cost Lynn's life at Dulles. Michael in Geneva. Along with your old friend, Pinwheel."

"I paid their Wànhuātǒng back with their hire."

"Taking pawns is ridiculous."

"It won't be pawns for long. After Geneva, they'll surmise that pawns don't play well for them."

"Their plans for the South China Sea worry me."

Silas shook his head. "Overt military expansion. That isn't this. They'll readjust after Geneva."

"I don't see how. They don't control any of the energy regions."

Silas sat. Elbows on his knees, he leaned in at the Russian. "Here's how." Derisive. "Your Kalaydoskop has always pushed in through Russia/the Soviet Union's overt arms and military assistance. American Kaleidoscope? Easy. We ride in with the economic and social development."

"What room does that leave China's Wànhuātǒng?"

"Rapid-built infrastructure. Their South China Sea aggression is a 'look how fast and unstoppable we are at building something from nothing' calling card."

Silas gave him a hard look.

Smug motherfucker knows.

"It will be China-engineered. China-built. It will come in the form of loans. They'll make them in Yen. You Russian morons were never a problem where the dollar stood. But the CCP can be."

"Then it is good you still work for me, mmm?"

"Kalaydoskop? Guess what? I'm not working for you. That died with my wife and my retirement. You know my radio call was bullshit. You're only here because you can't believe I'd work with you. You've only done this to Michael because you want to make sure I don't leave you in the dust."

"There can only ever be one winner between us."

"But that demands there are only two players."

"And, you presume you'll beat me? Silas?"

"I never lose."

"You lost the only woman both of us loved."

"You didn't love her."

"You know I did. How I did. In a way you never experienced."

Kolya rose to his feet. In the strange silver moonlight stippling through a thousand holes, gaps and spaces in the wooden cross-hatched beams of the patio's rooftop, through the rotted fragments dangling like the lowered flags of fallen kingdoms, he mimicked, in look and posture and form, a young man just turned forty.

Silas seemed to wilt and age in direct contrast.

When Kolya spoke, the years had left his voice. "You know in your hard poison heart Doris loved me. Before you. Alongside you—see, I can acknowledge her love for you, mistaken and unearned and unreturned in an authentic way, as it always was with you—to the end.

"You knew I was on that boat. You knew I had the means to save her life, and you prevented her."

"What you had was experimental! Communist fantasy. A horrid lure of false hope."

"*Was* experimental. It has been effective—proven effective—many times since. You chose tonight, the anniversary of that precious girl's death. To what?"

Silas's eyes flamed. He knew, suddenly and completely, like something he'd carefully brought with him into the Enchanted Forest, cupped and covered and precious in his hands. He'd thrust it out at Kalaydoskop, daring him to pull back the cover and only now, as

Kolya looked, Silas saw into the mirror of his soul and envisioned the answer the Russian put into words.

"To punish yourself. Like some kind of sacrifice so I won't reveal the world and how it is to Michael?"

Silas whipped out the pistol. Kalaydoskop barely looked at it. "I will be with her when you shoot me. If not tonight, mmm? The time you finally do. You've nourished yourself on the poisoned mushrooms of your fate since Tula. But when you die. Perhaps when I shoot you—"

How the hell'd he get his gun out?

"You'll never see Daria in the afterlife because there's no window to look up from the bottomless pit of a permanent Halloween... The dead drop?"

I could've handed the crap to you.

Silas gave a vacant nod.

👑 👑 👑

FOXTAIL FARM. Halloween night, 2002. The night is dark. Only three people are on the property. Doris—dying in her bed. Lynn—front door/side servant door: locked. Bolts thrown. Running. Locking the porch screen doors. Braces them with furniture. Locking the windows. Locking the shutters. Braces them with the fireplace andirons. Braces them with lamps. Frantic and crying and crazed.

Movement outside. Silas pounding. Silas enraged. Breaking glass.

Movement above.

"Mom! Stay in bed! Lock your door! Don't you move!"

Pounding. Smashing. "God dammit, girl! You open this house!"

Pulling. Pushing. Straining.

Wind blasts from the Chesapeake.

Tugging. Swearing. Shoulder plowing the round table in the dining room against French doors. An ax blade tearing the screen in the porch door.

"Damn you to hell, Lynn! I'm coming in! You stupid drunk!"

She grabs the shotgun from the corner. Where she shoved it.

Silas's eyes. Lynn's eyes. Double barrel eyes.

Wind howls down the chimney.

Mirrors. Doris. Upstairs corridor. Small. Frail. Her silk dressing gown, silk kimono style. Shear. Bridal length. Flows behind her, wraithlike. Papers. Letters, ribbon-tied. Diaries. Gathered in her silk-flowing arms.

Lynn. Terror and confusion. "What are you doing?! What have you got?! Back in your room! Lock the door! Mom-please!"

Doris drops the papers. They scatter at her feet.

The portrait watches alongside Lynn. Leering. Some pages flutter past the chandelier.

Lynn's eyes, red and inebriated; misunderstanding. The moment. Her mother. Her life.

Doris's eyes red and dying. Doris's eyes: begging forgiveness.

Lynn grabs the railing rushing toward—

Red Doris. The party. The dress. The portrait. Papers land at Lynn's feet.

Raging wind. The house bellowing, a creature brutalized and brutalizing.

At her feet. A letter written in Cyrillic.

Pounding. Splintering wood.

Lightning burning Lynn's brain: the utility porch/mud room!

"GO BACK, MOM!"

Lynn runs. Doris does not go back. Doris pulls the silken cord from around her waist. Her dressing gown falls open. She is only skin and skeleton.

Crash! Crash! Crash!

Lynn charges for her father breaking inside.

Doris ties a long loop in the silken cord. Weakly throws it at the chandelier. Once. Twice. Three times.

Crash! Crash! Craaack!

The fourth time the loop catches on a graceful iron, electric candelabra arm.

Black iron. White silk.

The top triangular panels of the utility room Dutch door explode in splinters. The back of an ax-head smashes through.

Lynn trips on her gin-blooded feet. Loses the shotgun. The shotgun hits butt first. Fires into the ceiling.

Lying there, Lynn can see Silas's bullet head thrust through. Mad bull eyes. Filled with fury. Filled with hate.

His hand plunges through the splintered hole. Fingers spidering. Snatching. Finding the bolt.

Doris sits on the rail. Her back to the chandelier. Doris drops one, two, three lit matches on the pages, the letters, the fragile, girlish, handwritten, dream and nightmare, hope, wish, confessional, prayer-full books. The other end of her dressing gown cord is fashioned into a second, smaller loop. A smaller loop cinched tightly around her neck.

The pages burn. Wills all of them burn. Doris watches the fire. Satisfied. She looks at her reflection in a wall mirror. So terribly sad for the girl she sees, the woman she became. Her eyes wander to the bottom of the tilted glass. To the reflection of the other Doris. The Red Doris who will never have to say goodbye.

The red dress. The indecipherable smile. The look of invitation to a secret.

The lips you kiss once and wish to kiss forever.

She leans back.

♔ ♔ ♔

THE OLD CARRIAGE HOUSE HOTEL was just that. The old carriage house for a Gothic mansion built on Dupont Circle in 1879. Converted to a boutique hotel, 2003. Known for its privacy. Discretion. Intimate rooms.

Within the upstairs turret room. A tipped over, half-empty bottle of gin on the floor.

Lynn buried her face in a down pillow as Roman Sayadov took her, thrusting from behind. Her screams into the pillow came back to him as ecstasy. Her flooding tears absorbed into the Egyptian cotton. Her naked body, slick and hot with fire—passion, and imagined fire relived—covered itself in gooseflesh.

No arousal.

Only memory.

Foxtail Farm taking a huge breath of air and spewing flame.

Lynn sobs. Deep. Uncontrollable. On hands and knees. Silas throws wide the bottom half of the Dutch door. The wind shoves from behind. Shoves Silas inside. Blasts past him. Blasts past Lynn, whipping/tangling hair. Blasts like a long-drawn breath for the mouth of the common room chimney flue. Greedily, it sucks it up. Then the chimney exhales into the house.

Silas grabs Lynn under her arms and yells in her face: "What have you done?!"

Doris emits a choking, anguished scream.

Silas throws Lynn against the wall. Tears stream her face. Somehow, she already knows, already sees her mother hanging.

Second sight comes more easily from the devil than from God when you hate yourself.

She wants to—but she doesn't sink. Lynn throws herself off the wainscotting. Plunges back for the foyer.

Her mother hangs above her, blowing in the wind. But she is not all that is blowing. The hanging is not the worst horror.

"You can't go up there!" She grabs her father.

OF ALL HIS CHILDREN, Silas knew Lynn was his most re-markable in every way. He loved her most dearly for this and for this most dreadfully.

Kolya, as always, had crushed him. Instead of walking directly back to his car, he crossed the ghostly theme park street, ravaged by time, consumed by the slow, creeping rage of ivy, to where he'd wheeled Lynn—too old to be in the stroller—to where the Lady in the Lake would always rise.

The water show. The dancing fountains.

Golden sword.

The upstretched arm.

A bathing suit made to look like diamond mail: the Lady in the Lake.

AFTER SERVICING THE DEAD DROP inside the castle, the place only he and Kalaydoskop know to look, after waiting for Kalaydoskop to get his hands off his wife, get away from his son, get away from Lynn, Silas pushes Lynn's stroller. Doris and Michael fall in on either side.

"Why did you take so long, Dad?" Michael.

"Did the balloon man give you that? It's a real bright red. Swell, huh?"

Michael's round face, upturned, parts inquisitive and bewildered. Silently tells Silas he knows his father saw the man. Saw the kiss.

Silas's face tells Michael they will go with this cover story. They will tell the story this way: they will not tell the story at all.

Music crescendos over the loudspeakers. The fountains dance and play.

"Daddy, Mommy ar'dy showed me." Lynn.

Michael needs to be helpful. "I didn't see it."

"I like it." Silas.

Doris says, "Let's watch it again."

Golden sword.

Upstretched arm.

The Lady in the Lake, water dripping from her diadem-crowned head. From her bathing suit chain-mail. False diamonds can also appear perfect. Without flaw.

Michael says, "If Arthur pulled the sword from the stone as Wart, how does the Lady in the Lake have it to give to him?"

Silas glances at Doris. Doris winks. She's got this. Silas beams at her.

He loves her.

He never hasn't.

He never could not.

Lynn chimes first. "The sword in the stone isn't Ex-calibur. Wart's sword in the stone got broken in a war against King Lot. I think it was King Lot. The Lady in the Lake gives King Arthur Excalibur."

Silas shows Doris white-wide eyes.

Doris says, "It's not in The Once and Future King.*"*

"Lynn. How do you possibly know that?" says Silas.

"I was looking for King Arthur pictures in Michael's World Book. *There was a picture of her, just like/almost like that. Michael read it to me. I remember it wasn't in your favorite book, Mommy. At least what you read us."*

"What did you learn?" Doris says.

"Merlin takes him to the Lake. But it's not the sword that's magic. I mean, it is, because it gave Arthur a way to see power like God sees power. And—" purely rote

memory— "the scabbard makes it so Arthur can't bleed, but he forgets to wear it."

"She's pretty," says Michael, his attention on the young park employee wet in her bathing suit.

Silas watches Doris crouch in front of Lynn. Doris says—and what she says is of utmost importance— "He'd never be able to forget the sheathe if he never drew Excalibur from it."

"King Arthur wouldn't have died if he hadn't fought." Lynn smiles, learning.

"And the Round Table and justice would have become the whole wide world," her mother tries to make all four of them understand.

Silas turns Lynn's stroller. He loves whole-world for the so-smart little girl. He says, "And the water will show us forth."

♛ ♛ ♛

PAGES SWIRL in a cyclone of fire. The silk catches first and fast. The banister and the walls spark and glow.

"Burn, please. Damn paper." Gasps. "Ignite." She chokes on smoke. "Lord, redeem me!"

Silas shakes from Lynn's grip. Fire rains. Wife and mother burns and—

I can't let her see Doris fall.

He viciously shoves Lynn back from the landing.

"Get out! Get out of this house!"

Silas rushes Lynn. Throws her to the bottom.

Gulping smoke. Gulping air. Gulping tears. Lynn flees.

Silas rushes to the top. Wades into the fire. The wind blows it everywhere and all around, and Doris—

"Doris!" He can't stop calling her name.

—blows and burns and spins and for an instant her eyes hold his as his hand closes around her fingertips. Her eyes are saying something. Her lips move. Smoke obscures, and she dies in the instant the silk cord snaps.

Silas loses the grip he never especially held. Doris crashes in flame and spark to the floor below.

Epilogue

I N BEIJING, CHENG SET examples. Four generals and six colonels, a mix of military and intelligence officers, were retired from Wànhuātǒng, Kaleidoscope. Retired themselves from their commands. Retired themselves from public sight. Their retirement included their families. Military units attached to China's Kaleidoscope were disbanded. Members scattered into different divisions. Cheng made sure none would come in contact again. Of the core one hundred eighteen intelligence officers who remained attached, he spoke to them of prizing *Dìng dīng jīngshén.*

Their new disposition.

New ethos.

A new indomitable will to toil zealously, beyond the best efforts of their task, until they embrace their work like the hammer fervently embraces the nail.

Cheng changed the Operation's name to reflect its new direction: K-范围, K-Scope.

Took zero credit. Removed K-Scope from targeting the American Kingstons. Removed them from targeting Kalaydoskop and his surrogates. Baku, in December, would remain; K-Scope would work to frustrate US and Russian intentions, and through them greater European petroleum, and gas control and supply. K-Scope would piggyback their operations on the government's burgeoning plans for global infrastructure dominance. K-Scope would move to dominate the energy supply developing in rare earth minerals.

"All of these things our enemies are aware of. All these things our enemies will seek to control in the turn of their kaleidoscope. Our goal, however, will not be to win their game. Our goal will only be to frustrate."

In the large briefing room where they assembled, Cheng Li-Qiang dimmed the lights. He illuminated the walls with a dozen panoramic photographs.

"Our enemies believe the world turns on the energy human beings purpose to the utility of task. They forget that the primary energy from which primary utility is born is the energy of human beings."

Bright upon the walls: fields of waving grain; farms of ripening fruit; plains of ranging cattle.

The photos faded out. The room pitched black. Cheng's voice resounded in the darkness.

"And the prime energy—the dominance over which will control all?"

He thumbed his remote. All four walls blazed a true and crystal white. A massive, single image now encased them all. The top of the world.

The Artic.

About the author

AWARD-WINNING NOVELIST MICHAEL FROST Beckner began a Hollywood career as writing assistant to Academy Award winner Barry Levinson on "Good Morning, Vietnam" and "Rain Man". In 1989, Beckner's script for "Sniper" launched a military-thriller franchise now on its tenth sequel. Three consecutive record-breaking spec script sales and three films later, Tony Scott directed Beckner's original screenplay "Spy Game." An international hit that paired Robert Redford and Brad Pitt as CIA partners and rivals, it is now a classic in the espionage genre.

The pilot for Beckner's CIA-based television drama "The Agency" for CBS, predicted Osama bin Laden's terror attack and the War on Terror four months before 9/11. In that series alone, Beckner would go on to predict three more international terror events.

Having penned close to 100 original screenplays, adaptations, and teleplays in the employ of every major film studio, television network, and cable outlet, he is a Hollywood institution.

As a commentator on American espionage, Beckner has appeared on CNN, Fox News, CBS News, TF1 in France, and as a featured guest of Bill Maher on HBO.